A DOG
WORTH
STEALING

WILLIAM CORBIN

A DOG WORTH STEALING

ORCHARD BOOKS

A DIVISION OF FRANKLIN WATTS, INC.

New York & London

Orchard Books
387 Park Avenue South
New York, New York 10016

Orchard Books Great Britain
10 Golden Square
London W1R 3AF England

Orchard Books Australia
14 Mars Road
Lane Cove, New South Wales 2066

Orchard Books Canada
20 Torbay Road
Markham, Ontario 23P 1G6

Orchard Books is a division of Franklin Watts, Inc.

First printing 1987

MANUFACTURED IN THE UNITED STATES OF AMERICA

Book design by Tere LoPrete

10 9 8 7 6 5 4 3 2 1

Library of Congress Cataloging-in-Publication Data
McGraw, William Corbin.
A dog worth stealing.
Summary: On a hike in the Pacific Northwest, Jud
unexpectedly acquires a lovable dog and in the process
learns some lessons about self-control.
[1. Dogs—Fiction. 2. Self-control—Fiction.
3. Oregon—Fiction] I. Title.
PZ7.M47855Do 1987 [Fic] 87-5795
ISBN 0-531-05712-7
ISBN 0-531-08312-8 (lib. bdg.)

The text of this book was set in 11/13 Janson.

To Eloise

A DOG
WORTH
STEALING

CHAPTER

1

Done it again, dummy, done it again—DONE IT AGAIN.

The load Jud Linden carried on his back was nothing; he could carry it all day, and *had*, many a time. But the load on his mind was trying to drive him into the ground as he strode among the towering trees. That peace that usually enveloped him on forest trails eluded him now, thanks to the relentless hammering of those words. Done it again, dummy—*done it again....*

Granite Ridge was behind him now, and here the wilderness began. It wouldn't end until the coastal mountains began their plunge to the thin strip of civilization along the craggy shores of southern Oregon. Home was a good four hours and eight or nine miles behind him. And where he was going—well, maybe he'd know when he got there.

The worn, discolored pack rode easily on his back as he moved among the endless firs and occasional hemlock or cedar, and he should have been at ease. But he could hear only the hammering of those words and see only Mattingly's bloody face. Mattingly bloody and scared as he backed away from a kid of barely sixteen to his seventeen, a kid he outweighed by maybe fifteen pounds. And Jud like some machine gone crazy, wishing to hell the other guys would grab him, hold him back, because he didn't have sense enough to stop himself.

Why? What was the whole dumb thing *for?* Because Mattingly was a mouth? Well, everybody knew that, but not everybody tried to shut it for him. Only Jud Linden did that. And only because he happened to come up to a bunch of guys just in time to hear Mattingly make a few remarks about Margie Freeman.

So *what?* Margie Freeman was nothing to him. Just one of the girls at school. Guys like Mattingly were always mouthing off like that when they had an audience. Macho stuff. But mostly they didn't expect anyone to believe them Probably Mattingly didn't either.

So who had to pop his big mouth open without a moment's thought and say, "Mattingly, that's a stinking lie!" Maybe it was and maybe it wasn't; all Jud knew for sure was that he didn't like hearing it. Naturally, Mattingly couldn't let that pass, so he said, "Figure you can *prove* it's a lie?"

No more was said. No time. No inclination, no breath to spare for words. Not with an explosion on the one hand and a struggle for survival on the other.

They didn't grab him until Mattingly had gone down. Tripped maybe, in his scramble to back off, but down all the same and in no hurry to get up. They said things to Jud while he stood pumping air into lungs that couldn't hold enough, but the words didn't seem to mean anything. He saw the way they looked at him, though—sideways, warily—as if he'd been a grenade or something that might blow up any moment. He'd seen that look before and it made him cringe. There may have been people who got their kicks out of making others afraid of them, but he wasn't one of those. It made him feel guilty instead, and ashamed, and led eventually to serious talks with his dad, to promises he deep-down meant to keep. Did keep—until something brushed against the inner hair trigger that set him off. The trigger marked Unfairness.

The last go-round, when he'd made the Solemn Promise, Dad had looked, and sounded, a lot more serious than the time before that. "Dammit, Jud," he'd said, "I'm worried about you. Where's all this going to end? And *why?* That's what I just don't get. You're no bully, no troublemaker; you're a good, decent, conscientious guy, and a pleasure to have around. Nobody knows that any better than I do. But every so often you blow like Mount St. Helens and somebody gets hurt."

Jud had offered no defense, and Dad went on. "Boys are expected to get into stupid fights. I did my share of it. But *think*, Jud. In just a couple of years you'll be a grown man in the eyes of the law, and grown men *aren't* expected to do the kind of thing you've been doing. They do it and they get in trouble—bad trouble. I can't believe you want that; you're too smart!"

In the end Jud had made the promise. Keep his cool. Keep his fists in his pockets. Stay out of trouble. . . .

So what was he doing now? Heading into the Kalmiopsis Wilderness, far from any marked trail, alone, nothing but his compass and his maps to guide him. Running away from himself. Dumb idea, naturally. But at least in the wilderness there'd be nobody to get in trouble *with*.

And that brought up another aspect of his general overall dumbness: He wasn't supposed to be doing this at all. *No-*

body was supposed to head into the wilderness alone. If he hadn't made a detour around the trailhead where hikers were supposed to check in the rangers would have turned him back with a few well-chosen words. The Kalmiopsis was rough country—beautiful, interesting, but rough. No easy trails, mapped and marked. Few trails at all. No long vistas of stately trees and mountain crests, no long reaches of river easily followed, the way it was over along the Rogue. Here there was heavy cover beneath the trees, abrupt rocky ravines, deep and treacherous. You easily could break an ankle or a leg.

These mountains, part of the Siskiyous, were older than time, and by time they had been altered in fantastic ways. Everywhere rocks known locally as "buckskin boulders"— really peridotite further metamorphosed here and there into serpentine—which were glossy, slick looking, often bright green. Beautiful to look at but treacherous underfoot. Then too the hiker had to share the wilderness with such full-time residents as the brown bear and the rattlesnake. One hazard at least posed no problem for Jud—the poison oak that flourished among the rocks and on the sides of ravines, often just where a person needed a handhold. Through some genetic quirk Dad had passed along to Jud a complete immunity to the violent allergic reaction of most human skin after contact with the plant. Allergy or not, there were perils enough in this vast wilderness to justify the Forest Service rule that required each hiker to have at least one companion who could go for help if need be.

Jud's companion would of course have been Dad, and if Dad had only kept his promise Jud wouldn't be pushing along now, deeper into the wilderness with every stride, because he was too hard-headed to turn back. He could even make a case for blaming everything on Dad, including flying off the handle with Mattingly.

The fact was that he and Dad had been planning a five-day hike into the Kalmiopsis ever since Christmas. On the weekends Dad was home—and mighty few they were—they'd refurbished their gear, replacing a worn item here and there, packaged a fresh supply of homemade jerky and granola along with dried foods ordered from catalogs, checked everything over about eight times, packed and repacked their trail packs. Most carefully packed of all were their oilskin map cases containing the latest topographical maps the county and Forest Service had to offer. These were stowed in compartments with outside flaps, easy to get at, at the bottom of the packs.

No run-of-the-mill hike, it was to have been their celebration of Jud's sixteenth birthday. In recognition that the day May 31 was a sort of milestone, the turning of a corner, they had agreed Jud would be the sole navigator. Dad would take his own maps, of course, and compass, but he wouldn't even look at them unless Jud made some kind of miscalculation and had to ask for help.

The big day was on a Friday, and on the Wednesday evening just preceding, the phone call had come. "I'm in Seattle," Dad had said, "and I'd rather take a broken nose than say what I've got to say." What he had to say was that he'd been in the wrong place at the right time and got stuck with a run over into Idaho with a load of mining machinery. Couldn't possibly get home before the first of the week.

Jud had nearly lost his cool then and there, yelling into the phone, "No! You can't do this! Look—you could get out of it—there must be a way!"

"I could get out of it," came the answer. "But dammit,

Jud, I can't afford to. The mine over there's shut down till they get the stuff, and they're going bananas. Offered double rates if I leave tonight and go straight through."

Jud's next howl of protest was chopped off when Dad's voice took on a brittle edge that showed he was holding in. "That'll do! You're going to start bein' a grown man come Friday—start now instead."

It took some doing, but Jud had kept his mouth shut. Dad was making an effort too, trying now for a lighter tone. "Once I've made my first million I'll take off any time the spirit moves me. Meanwhile, nose to the grindstone— baby needs a new pair of shoes."

An unfortunate choice of words. He didn't really mean *the* baby, but Jud chose to interpret it that way, and he felt as if he might explode. Couldn't anybody ever think of anything but the blasted *baby?* He made his face go rigid as a carving and thrust the wall phone's receiver toward Carla, who was sitting right there at the kitchen table furiously concentrating on her sewing—eternal *baby clothes*— trying to pretend not to hear what Jud was saying and that she wasn't burning to grab the phone and speak to her dear *husband.*

She took the phone, looking up at Jud with that sort of shy, halfway scared expression that drove him up the wall. Did she think he was about to slug her? The last thing he heard as he strode to the kitchen door and through it into the night was her small breathless voice: "Victor—oh yes —it's good to hear yours too. . . . !"

Victor! Why couldn't she for God's sake call him Vic like everybody else? *Vic*-tor, he mimicked silently, and let his legs propel him uncaringly down toward the creek. The stars were out and the air was soft with promises of summer, but it was the blackest night of his life and it could, for all he cared, have been pouring rain.

He hadn't known it then, but the next afternoon it was to be old Mattingly's bad luck to cross Jud Linden's path at the worst of all possible times.

He knew it all too well the day after that, his birthday, when he set off into the wilderness alone. Luckless Mattingly had taken a beating at least in part because Jud Linden was teed-off at his old man. Well—maybe so—but it never would have happened if Dad hadn't gone back on his promise. So didn't that sort of cancel out his own broken promise? Something way inside faintly murmured that it didn't, but he was nowhere near admitting it.

In the same manner he wasn't listening to any faint murmurs about Carla either. Maybe he hadn't been exactly polite the night before when he told her he was going on the hike by himself—but dammit, she bugged him so he hardly knew what he was saying. She'd looked quickly up at him with scared cow eyes that were too big for her face, her busy hands going suddenly motionless. After a moment she dropped her eyes again, disengaged her needle, sticking it into the pin cushion that was supposed to look like a tomato, folded the garment she'd been working on and put it in her basket. Still looking down, she said, "Do you—do you think you ought to? I mean, would your dad . . ."

"It's got nothing to do with him."

She stood, carried the basket to a cupboard, and put it away while Jud's eyes followed resentfully. Why, he asked himself yet again, if Dad had to get married, couldn't he have picked somebody his own age? But no, he'd had to go for this—this *stranger* ten years younger than he was and only ten years older than Jud. Which made her about twenty-six, but she looked about twenty, which was his sister's age.

And that was another thing that bugged him. In baby-talk days Elinor had been his Nory—revised to Snory somewhere along the line—for years his chief companion and playmate. Then, when he was eight and their mother left for California to "find herself," whatever that meant, she had promoted herself from sister to mother. She made him mad as fire half the time, making him wash, wear clean clothes to school, mind his table manners and his language, and refusing flat-out to believe he had already done his homework or that there hadn't been any in the first place. She read to him and sang to him, comforted him when he was hurt, and he had wallowed in many a daydream about the spectacular vengeance he would wreak on anyone so foolhardy as to mistreat her.

In those days Dad was driving a logging truck for Weyerhauser Lumber, making wages, and was home every evening, but half the time he might as well have been somewhere else. He'd sit for hours in front of the TV not really watching, just thinking, brooding, seldom talking if he didn't have to. He provided food, but mostly it was pizza from Tony's up in Cave Junction, or deli stuff from a place in tiny O'Brien on the Redwood Highway in the other direction, toward the California line.

After about a year of that, something happened—Jud never learned what—and Dad had begun to come to life, talking, even joking as in the old days, and he began planning and working toward saving money, borrowing more, and getting a truck of his own. Best of all, though, he started taking Jud on trail hikes—near home at first, then farther and farther. West toward Chetco Peak south of the Kalmiopsis, east along the Rogue, south along the Applegate, anyplace they could get to in the pickup where the road and civilization ended. Dad had learned map reading, navigation, and wilderness survival in Korea when the Army decided to make a surveyor of him. He'd passed this lore along as fast as Jud could take it in, and from the time

Jud was nine until the present they calculated they'd covered at least a thousand miles, over easy country and rough, good weather and bad.

Dad had tried at first to interest Snory in these expeditions and got the response that he called "twenty-four-carat, undiluted, one hundred percent Snory," and he quoted it every chance he got. "By the time I'm ninety-five I'll probably have walked nine hundred and ninety-five thousand miles just between the stove and the kitchen sink. So I plan to *sit* whenever I get the chance, which is right now. You guys go and play Dan'l Boone and leave me here to do it."

Dad seemed to be satisfied with that, and anything was all right with Jud, just so nothing got in the way of hiking. For a long time nothing did, and that, in Jud's mind, was the way things were meant to be, the way they should go on being forever. So of course they didn't. They began to change when Dad finally, as he put it, "borrowed from hell and the hereafter" to buy the nearly-new tractor-trailer rig and began making trips that took him away from home anywhere from a day or two to a week. By then Snory was in high school, had taught herself to cook simple meals, and cracked the whip over Jud to make him hike the mile and a half to O'Brien for supplies. She often made him do it even after she reached sixteen and got a license to drive the pickup. When he complained, she would say something like, "I've got six other things to do—and anyway what's a lousy three miles to the great conqueror of the world's wildernesses?" If he got stubborn about it she was likely to do what she called her "Nashville sound," an imitation of the country-music performers Dad liked to watch. "Tell ya what, Jud good buddy, you got a eeeasy choice. You hike, you eat; you don't hike, you don't eat." She could carry it on indefinitely and in the end she always wore him down, made him laugh, and off to the store he'd go. Often he'd threatened to get a bike but somehow never did. After all, he was a hiker. Over easy ground he could make forty miles in a day, hardly working up a sweat.

And things had gone right on changing—never for the better. The next ax to fall—two years or so ago—was Carla. She changed Dad, which was bad enough, but even worse, she changed Snory. At first his sister had been on his side, resenting the intrusion of a stranger into their life, but in what seemed no time at all she'd swung traitorously around. The two got thick as thieves, and Snory took to giving him tart little lectures: ". . . If you can't stop snarling at her in the name of common decency, you could at least do it for Dad's sake!" That kind of lecture. The two had got even more unbearable about six months ago when Carla's pregnancy was announced. They went on and on about what was going on inside of dear Carla, and about exercises and natural birth, and *breathing*, and maternity clothes and nursing and whether Pampers were better than the other kind and a million other such things until Jud wanted to howl like a coyote and tear things apart.

Because of all that it was almost a relief instead of the blow it might have been when about a month ago Snory had miraculously landed a summer job over at Ashland at the Shakespearean Festival. She had left at once and probably, Jud speculated gloomily, wouldn't be back much anymore because in the fall she'd stay there and be a freshman at Southern Oregon State College.

Relief or not, her departure meant that things would never be the same again. For long intervals there was nobody there but him and Carla. Carla and her sewing. Carla and her silly attempts to tell him how great it would be to have a little sister or brother. Carla's insistence on making conversation when it should have been plain to see he wasn't interested. City-bred Carla who was afraid of being alone after dark in this isolated place while Jud was off tramping in the woods somewhere and leaving her alone for hours. After all, he didn't do it more than once or twice a week, and he *did* have to stay in shape and keep an edge on his trail skills.

One thing he had to admit, though: She never said anything to Dad when he came home about the times she'd been alone and fearful. But after all, it was her own stupid fault they didn't have a dog to stand guard for her. Lord knows Jud had argued for one often enough. But no—poor little Carla was scared of dogs too, the story being that some mutt had nipped her once when she was three years old. It was unfair. It was probably the unfairest thing in the whole bundle. Just one little word from little old Carla and Dad had dug his heels in. No. No dog. So Jud was under sentence to grieve forever for old Bigfoot, the massive Labrador-Dane and friend of his childhood who had met with sudden death on the highway scarcely a month before Carla's appearance on the scene. Patient old Bigfoot whom he'd ridden all over the place like a pony. Bigfoot, who had grabbed him by the tail of his T-shirt many a time and dragged him away from the bank of a stream swollen in springtime, or from the county road which teenage drivers often turned into a dragstrip. Bigfoot, who would lie still for however long it took while a silly little kid clutched his massive neck and sobbed into its silken folds until he could face the world again.

Just where along the line the fighting had begun Jud wasn't sure, and the why of it was more uncertain still. It could have been the time way back when he was eight, not long after Mom had gone her way. An older kid—Vinnie somebody—who had lived up the road a way, had pinned him down, sat on him, wouldn't let him move. He was laughing, pretending he was just horsing around, but Jud knew bullying when he came up against it, and the pressure built inside him. He could still feel that pressure when he thought about it—growing, growing—like the stress level along a fault line deep in the earth. Then something slipped and the earthquake struck. This restraint, this weight, those arms that held him powerless, could not be tolerated for even one more instant, and he had exploded. He simply had to break free, whatever the price. Injury meant nothing. Pain meant nothing. Death was just a word. A long time later he'd read somewhere that the violently insane are so hard to subdue because they hold nothing back. No ounce of strength remains unused. No conscience holds them back, no fear.

But Jud wasn't crazy. Well, maybe something like it, but only momentarily. It was a disturbing thought, and he was careful not to dwell on it.

Busy not dwelling on it, particularly in connection with yesterday and Mattingly, he took his eyes from the ground ahead of his steadily moving feet and glanced skyward because a slanting ray of sunlight had flashed across his face. The first such ray in many minutes, meaning either that there was a thinning of the forest cover above or that he had passed beyond whatever west-lying ridge had been blocking the sun from his path. Not only that, the streak of light was saying something else. In a split second he had it and a whispered "Damn!" broke the profound silence.

The sun was in the wrong place. Which meant either that he'd veered off course, or that more time had passed than he had any idea of while he'd been doing the goof-off act, thinking about all his problems, thinking about everything in God's world but what he should have been thinking about. Such as where was he—how had he got here—and what lay up ahead?

He called himself a lot of uncomplimentary names—but silently. The wilderness didn't deserve to be profaned by the ranting of a half-baked sorry excuse of a hiker who had broken the first commandment: know at all times where you are! It might be all right to relax, even to goof off a little if you were following a trail, no matter how sketchily marked, or following a stream or a mountain crest with landmarks on all sides. But in the wilderness—never. And now he'd done it. For the first time ever he was glad Dad wasn't along.

CHAPTER

2

At least, Jud thought grimly, he could pay strict attention to commandment Number two: Never panic. He'd strayed, but he wasn't lost. The thing to do was to backtrack, using his compass, his maps, and above all—his *head*. Casting around, he spotted a mossy boulder, about chair height, shrugged out of his pack, which he leaned against the rock, and sat down.

First order of business—a snack and a drink. From an outside pocket of the pack he took a bar of "Dad's Unpatented, Unguaranteed Home-made Pemmican" and gnawed thoughtfully on it while unzipping the map case. Opening the map, he began studying it, alternating bites of pemmican with sips of water from his one-pint polyethylene bottle, glancing occasionally at the compass, which he had set on the rock for steadiness.

Now that the sound of his own footfalls had ceased, the silence of the forest seemed to swell, to intensify, to embrace the universe. It seemed absolute, like total deafness. But only for a few moments, then slowly, all but imperceptibly, the silence fragmented. High above, the air was on the move, sliding through the treetops with shy apologetic sighs. From still farther aloft in the unseeable sky came, fainter than a breath, the screek of a sail-planing hawk, and in a moment the answering screek of its mate. Nearer at hand but faint enough to seem only an imagining, the trickle of water over rock. From somewhere else—direction impossible to pinpoint—the drone of bees at work on early wildflowers, maybe even on the kalmiopsis, the rare rhododendron-like shrub for which the wilderness was named. He leaned down to zip the bottle back into its compartment and suddenly froze, the bottle still in his hand. Then he came slowly erect, listening intently, head moving from side to side like a sonar screen, seeking to pinpoint a new sound.

It was a baffling sound, an alien sound, one that didn't belong here in the wilderness, and after only a moment it stopped. The forest silence closed in again. Jud waited, breathing shallowly through his mouth, at the same time playing the strange sound back through his mind. Had it been something dropped? Something that bounced once or twice? Something metallic? Metal meant human presence. Other hikers? Didn't seem likely. Few hikers out this early in the season. And the wilderness was vast; the chance of meeting someone was about like stars colliding. Anyway, hikers didn't go around dropping things—and even if they did the things would fall more likely on soft ground than on rocks. Besides, the sound hadn't been like metal against rock. More like metal against wood.

He waited, and just as he was deciding it wasn't going to happen again, it did. This time it went on a bit longer but was no easier to identify. He frowned and squinted with the effort to hear better. This time, along with the metallic sound there was something else. Not metal, not rock, not wood—nothing like that. More like a sound that . . . yes, that was it—a sound that came from a throat. Animal or human. Human! It had to be; animals don't bang things with metal. What then? A cry, a moan, a groan?

The metallic sound stopped but the other went on, intermittently, like . . . Like spasms? Spasms of pain? Quickly Jud replaced map and compass, got to his feet, and shrugged into the pack.

Another commandment was operating now: Always go to the aid of anyone in trouble. Never mind studying anymore about where he'd gone wrong; he could come back to this spot later and take up where he'd left off. Unsheathing his knife, he made a small gash at eye level in the bark of the redwood sapling that grew beside the boulder he'd been sitting on. Sighting beyond it in the direction from which the sounds were coming, he made note of a downed tree, broken roots in the air, about sixty yards off, and headed toward it. Arriving there, he made another compass reading, another bark slash, and went on. His watch told him it was nearly four o'clock. Four hours or more of daylight left. So whatever happened he'd have to camp in the woods tonight and Carla would be spending the night alone for sure. It would really be a break to have the excuse that he'd been helping somebody in trouble.

At the next trail-marking spot he stopped again to listen. Nothing. Maybe whoever it was had lost consciousness and was unable to groan or to . . . To what? To bang whatever the metal thing was. That was it! The banging was a signal for help! But if whoever it was had to signal it meant he'd come out here alone, same as Jud. If that was so, why?

The answer he came up with for that one wasn't what

you'd call comforting. A fugitive. Escaped convict. He shook his head impatiently to dislodge this flight of imagination, took a sight on a huge moss-mottled boulder up ahead, and pressed on. Arriving, he scraped moss away to form an X and listened again. Nothing at first, then suddenly the two sounds together. Clearer now. He was closer, of course, but not that much closer, so the reason had to be a change in the lay of the land. He'd been climbing, not steeply but steadily, and now the ground was beginning to slope away ahead of him. He'd come to the top of a low ridge and the sounds were reaching him more easily. He strained his ears as intently as if his life depended on it—which maybe it did, for all he knew.

The sounds were repeated, but only for long enough to send him a new message: that moan was no moan at all, it was a whine. A dog whine! And it came, as best he could judge, from no farther away than five or six hundred yards. Now Jud's mind raced like a propeller out of water. What for the Lord's sake would a dog be doing way out here? No serious hiker would even consider bringing a dog along. For one thing, it would mean packing extra food where every ounce of pack weight was important. Furthermore, a dog would leave traces of himself unburied, a thing no good hiker would do. And a dog was likely to go charging off on the scent of an animal, leaving a path of destruction, mashing or breaking precious plants that grew nowhere else, scaring the daylights out of every animal in earshot.

Whoever had brought the dog, therefore, was not a hiker. Certainly he wasn't a resident, because there weren't any in the wilderness. Unless . . . Well, he could be a hermit, maybe, and a hermit might have a dog. But even a hermit, surely, would want to be a little nearer to civilization. So what did that leave? Nothing very reassuring. *Anybody* could walk into the wilderness. As he started on he found himself moving with extra caution, careful not to betray his presence with undue disturbance of the undergrowth as he passed through it, keeping a close eye on his feet lest he dislodge a loose rock that would in turn dislodge others.

His course led him down into yet another of the deep rocky ravines so common to the Kal, and as he climbed laboriously out of it he was so intent on remaining quiet and unseen that he neglected to observe that the light on all sides was growing brighter. So when his head suddenly emerged into sunlight he instinctively crouched, pulling back into the ravine like a turtle into its shell. Before him lay a small clearing irregularly shaped and covering roughly an acre. Stumps here and there showed that someone had partially cleared it, leaving an occasional bush or small tree. In between these were masses of a vivid green shrub unknown to him.

It wasn't the horticultural effects that captured his attention after the first fleeting moment, it was what lay beyond, at the far end of the more-or-less rectangular clearing. He stared, eyes wide, and stared some more. There at the far end, with the forest curling around it, stood a tent and about fifty feet behind it a privy. The tent was a big olive-drab one, like an army tent, and it had been there for a long time. This he could tell from the fact that it had been erected on a wooden platform which extended from the edges of the tent for about four feet on the sides and back, perhaps ten feet on the front, and the rough boards the platform was made of had seen more than one winter in this place. At the edge of the platform facing him were three crude steps.

It was those steps that were occupying the undivided attention of the only living creature in this unlikely wilderness scene—and it was that creature which instantaneously captured the attention of Jud Linden. It was a dog—a German shepherd, the most beautiful he had ever seen—with an almost completely black coat glinting in the sun like new-mined coal. He was on the ground, his tail wagging furiously as he toiled with the dedicated energy of a pyramid builder to push an object up the steps. Now and then he uttered a whine, high or low as the spirit moved him, and now and then the object made its own sound—somewhere between a clank and a clatter. Not until the dog, in a movement almost too fast to be seen, switched his point of attack from below to above could Jud see what was clattering. It was a battered aluminum saucepan, and the dog was above it now, standing on the platform and reaching down with his forepaws, scrabbling furiously at the pan, which was already on the second step. In a few frantic moments he got the pan safely to the first step from the top. His next lightning move was to flip himself back to the ground where, using the side of his head only, he pinned the pan against the top step and gradually maneuvered it upward.

During all these scientific operations the dog alternately panted and shut his mouth to concentrate on the next delicate phase of the performance. Jud caught himself feeling breathless, wanting to pant in sympathy. He couldn't have taken his eyes from the spectacle if a bear had ambled out of the woods and tapped him on the shoulder. It was all he could do to refrain from cheering a few moments later when, with a final and triumphant flip of his muzzle, the dog sent the pan sailing over the top to land with a clatter on the platform itself.

For a few seconds he stood looking down at the pan, still panting, then sat down and peered around in a half circle, as if hoping for applause. Jud could now see that his massive chest and belly were somewhere between tawny and silver. He was too far away to see any other markings, but nothing detracted from his first impression that this animal was the handsomest he'd ever seen of a handsome breed. More than that, there had to be extraordinary intelligence. How many dogs could there be who invented games—with *rules*—and then meticulously obeyed the rules! None that Jud had ever known or heard about. Obviously the dog could have seized the pan in his jaws at any moment and placed it anywhere he liked. But that was against the rules. No jaws allowed.

Lost though he was in admiration, Jud hadn't stopped using his brain. It told him that now the mystery was solved, now that he knew nobody stood in need of rescue, the sensible thing to do was to get out of here, to backtrack along the trail he'd marked, and go on from there. But he didn't want to do the sensible thing; he wanted to go on watching, to see if the game was over or if this was only half-time.

It was half-time. The dog suddenly rose to all fours again and stood peering down at the pan, ears pricked forward interestedly as if thinking I wonder what *that* thing is for! Then with the precise economical motion of the true athlete, he flipped the pan back down to the bottom of the steps.

Jud choked back his burst of laughter and turned it into a mere snort. No human at that distance would have heard it, but the dog did. His head snapped up, ears erect, hind legs bent in the characteristic half-crouch of the shepherd, muzzle moving this way and that as he tested the air. Then came a sound that set things to crawling inside Jud's stomach. It was a low-pitched growl of such menacing ferocity that it was almost possible to imagine that some genii had snatched away the playful animal of only a moment ago and put this fearsome creature in his place. Even at sixty or seventy yards Jud could see the slash of white across the black muzzle. A mouthful of teeth that could tear flesh and splinter bone with ease.

Jud had time for that one quick look and then things began happening with rocket speed. Like a jeans-clad jack-in-the-box, a young woman popped out of the tent, long reddish hair swinging wildly across her face as she tried to look in all directions at once. Then she snapped two sharp words at the dog. Jud couldn't make the words out, but it seemed as if one must have been the dog's name, the other a command.

The dog must have heard the command a split second before Jud did, because he launched himself from the platform like a black torpedo, not toward Jud's hiding place but the opposite way, and in a second or two disappeared into the forest behind the tent, a movement that Jud viewed with a kind of horrible fascination. He couldn't kid himself that the dog had goofed, gone the wrong way. Fat chance! This smart, beautiful, playful animal that he'd have given his soul to have for his own was a guard dog, and from the look of it he'd been trained to stay out of sight, to patrol the place when ordered to, staying under cover while he did it. How long would it take him to locate this particular target and to . . . to do whatever else he'd been trained to do? Five minutes? One minute? Thirty seconds?

Like a pheasant flushed from cover, Jud exploded into action. If he'd had the wings of a pheasant he'd have flown. As it was, he had only one chance: Get up a tree. *Fast.*

The first tree that caught his frantic eye was a fair-size maple with branches that looked reachable at the top of a leap. It stood about fifty feet away at the edge of the clearing, so he'd be plainly visible to anyone at the tent.

But this was no time for eeny-meeny-miney-mo and he hurled himself toward it at full-tilt, writhing like a desperate Houdini at the same time to get rid of the backpack. He had to. It could easily bang into a branch at the crucial point of his leap. A picture tormented him while he struggled —of himself hanging partway up, legs dangling within reach of . . . At the last possible moment the pack thumped to the ground behind him and he grabbed at the lowest branch which, close up, looked at least twenty feet up. He missed with one hand, latched on with the other. Pain seared his shoulder with the fierce effort it took to pull his weight higher.

When he reached the point where he could get his feet onto a branch and cling to the trunk with one arm—the one that didn't hurt—he looked down. No dog yet. He shifted his gaze quickly to the tent. No woman either. And now, from this height, he could see what he hadn't seen before: along one side of the tent was a rope stretched between two poles. On it hung two well-worn pairs of jeans that couldn't possibly have belonged to the young woman —to any woman. Somewhere around there was a man. A *big* man.

All this took only a few seconds, and it took even less for his eyes to focus on those bright green plants that grew all over the clearing in such profusion—plants with narrow spiky leaves. Plants he'd seen many times in photographs. Marijuana!

A second after that a shadow moved out from among the shadows at the edge of the ravine where he had lain hidden so briefly a time ago. The dog circled Jud's tree once, nose to the ground, then backed off a few feet, slowly raised his majestic head, and looked into Jud's eyes. He was even more handsome than Jud had thought, and when the blood stopped hammering his ears quite so hard, he uttered the most idiotic set of words he'd ever put together in his life. "*Good* dog. We could be friends, you and me!" The alert ears twitched ever so briefly. Message received. But the dark eyes never left the face of the stranger in the tree. Not even when the dog slowly crouched lower, lower still, and at length was lying down, relaxed as a revolver is relaxed when it's in a holster.

CHAPTER
3

For perhaps two minutes boy looked at dog, dog looked back, and boy at least wondered what was about to happen next. Then he grinned as his sense of the ridiculous took over. However many birthdays he might have, he thought, the sixteenth was the one he'd remember. On how many other days would he lose his way and get chased up a tree by a ferocious dog on the edge of a marijuana plantation in the middle of a wilderness?

Grin still in place, he spoke softly. "Hey, boy—don't you reckon you and me could find something better to do than *this?*"

If he hadn't been watching so closely he wouldn't have caught the tiny twitch of scalp and ears that was a rudimentary response, meaning that the friendliness in his tone was heard and understood. More than that, the jaws parted, the tongue came out in the start of a pant. Instantaneously the tongue withdrew, jaws closed as if the dog had suddenly remembered he was supposed to stay at attention. He looked a little embarrassed about it, like a sentry caught in a yawn.

Something about this little exchange—if it could be called that—told Jud that this dog wasn't exactly a veteran in the guard business. Besides, closer inspection showed the animal was younger than he'd thought. Full-grown all right, but not as massive as he'd be in another year. Old Bigfoot hadn't reached full size until the third year.

Time for idle speculation ended abruptly then when his eye caught movement in the direction of the tent. The woman emerged and was crossing the clearing in a purposeful manner that Jud found, to say the least, disquieting. She wore jeans and a faded red sweater, and she carried a rifle with both hands out straight in front, in a sort of present-arms position. Obviously she wasn't at ease with it.

In the sun her hair seemed more red than before, and not altogether clean. She looked about Carla's age, but more strongly built. As she neared the tree the dog stood up, watching her and Jud in turn. He made no sound. Jud tried to swallow to moisten his dry throat, but there wasn't much of anything to swallow. He tried sneering at himself; she wasn't likely to shoot him out of the tree like a squirrel or something. But how did he know? People who grew marijuana in places like this might do anything. There were plenty of stories about potshots taken at intruders—even officers in helicopters.

But what could he do? He could hardly be more helpless than he was, facing a gun and a dog both. Any second he'd have to say something, explain himself. He could make up some yarn about having got lost from his dad and some other men who weren't far away. Other ideas presented themselves, but a lot depended on this woman. Would she swallow a lot or only a little? Hardly a minute passed before he had the chance to find out. Halting a few yards away from his tree, she shifted the rifle to point in his direction and scowled up at him, narrowing her eyes which a trick of the light revealed as amazingly blue. Then she spoke in a voice not really high-pitched but of a timbre that seemed to belong to a girl his own age. She, he knew at once, was acting a part. "A'right, mistuh, just you tell me yoh name an' what you doin' hyeh!" A second passed and she added, "Foh I blast a *hole* in ya."

Her voice had a husky edge to it, not unpleasant, and the twang of her speech was much like Snory's "Nashville sound," only this was the real thing.

Probably because danger has a way of sharpening the wits, Jud knew in that moment that this woman was even more insecure than he was. More than that, there was something strange about her, something not quite normal. Not retarded, more like . . . The closest he could come was "childlike." As if she'd grown to be a woman while her mind refused to grow too.

Of course, all he had to go on was that one speech. Tough talk. But it didn't sound right. It sounded more like a girl's imitation of tough talk in a western movie.

Whether he was right about all this or not, the safe thing would be to go along with whatever she wanted. "Well, ma'm," he said—wouldn't hurt to be polite—"I sure don't want a hole in me. Name's Jud, and I'm here because . . ."

"Well, *hey!*" She sounded not only surprised but relieved. Pleased even. "You just a *kid*." It sounded like kee-ud.

He could almost have said the same about her, because these words too had a childlike sound. He nodded vigorously. "I'm fourteen, ma'm. Big for my age." He'd have said thirteen if he'd thought he could get away with it.

She lowered the rifle butt to rest on the ground. A good sign. "Only foh'teen!" she said more with admiration than anything else, as if fourteen was a remarkably clever thing to be. Then she apparently recalled the role she was playing and scowled abruptly with eyes narrowed in suspicion. "Mebbe so, but how's come you way out here snoopin' 'round, spyin' on folks? You speak up now. Pronto!"

Jud would have bet that "pronto" wasn't part of her ordinary vocabulary. But he obeyed. "I was about to tell you, ma'm. I'm not spying, I'm lost. Got lost yesterday from my Boy Scout troop, and when I tried to find them I must've gone the wrong way, and I called and called, and ran a lot and fell down, and then it got dark and I had to get in my sleeping bag and darn near froze anyway, and I slept some but mostly I just lay there and listened to the bears and things and was scared."

He was working up to trying out a little quaver in his voice when good sense told him to shut up. His act must have worked anyway, because she lifted the rifle and set the safety lock. He could hear it click. Then she leaned the weapon against her side and cocked a hip to keep it in place. She seemed barely able to wait until he called a halt to his rambling tale. "*I* got lost when I was a little kid— that was back east—and they didn't find me for three days. I like to *died!*"

She paused for breath and Jud was quick to grab his chance. "It sure isn't any fun being lost, lady, and I'd really appreciate it if you'd point me in the right way out of this wilderness. All I want to do is get back home."

"Come on down outa that tree an' likely I'll do it." To his surprise she followed this with a giggle. "Um gettin' a crick in m'neck talkin' up at you like this."

"Sure would like to. Getting a cramp in my leg. But how's your dog going to feel about it?"

"Won't hurt you none, less'n I tell him to. Git on down now."

Jud moved to the next limb down and cast a wary eye toward the dog, who was watching with the appearance of mildly enjoying the performance. Once his tail wagged —not so much a wag as a twitch. Maybe a twitch and a half. Jud grinned in response. It would have been hard not to. There was something about this dog, some attraction beyond his dark beauty and the high intelligence that shone from his eyes. Jud couldn't put his finger on it, but it was there, a spirit of—what? *Willingness*, maybe. Willingness to do what was expected of him, and more. Willingness to respond, to react, to *communicate* to the best of his ability. Jud gave his attention to reaching the bottom limb and swinging from it to the ground, telling himself he couldn't possibly perceive so much about a dog in so short a time, and from such a vantage point as halfway up a tree.

"Well, I swear!" The woman was regarding him with fascination. "You purely are a big one for foh'teen!"

"Runs in the family," Jud said. Good thing he hadn't tried for thirteen. Even so, a change of subject was in order. "That sure is one fine dog you've got."

"He ain't just fer looks; he's a *century* dog!" There was that childlike note again, as in the giggle. But what was a century dog? Was that breed a hundred years old—or what?

His puzzlement must have showed because she said helpfully, "*You* know—like in 'Halt, who goes there?' "

"Oh. Is he on sen—uh—is he on duty now?" It wouldn't have been kind, he thought, to correct her.

"Not now he ain't. I tooken' him off."

Jud thought back. "How? I didn't hear you say anything to him."

Now her eyes lighted with glee. "Din't say nothin'. I give a signal."

"Oh." He seemed to be saying "oh" a lot. "What was the signal?"

She hesitated, then gave in. Secrets were no fun if you didn't tell them to somebody. Smiling mysteriously, she lowered her right arm to her side, hand extended, palm downward, and waggled it twice at the wrist.

"And that did it?"

"Yup."

"So he's off duty now?"

"Sure is." Then she frowned, no doubt remembering that *she* was on duty. "But don't try nothin' smart. Another signal an' he'll be a-watchin' you again."

Jud hastened to reassure her. "Hadn't even *thought* of it. I was just going to ask if I could pet him a little."

He was sure she was about to assent when she shook her head violently. "No way! Nobody allowed to pet him. Not even me."

He tried to sort out what was behind this strange outburst. There was definitely a note of resentment in the last part of it. Maybe he could fan that flame a little. "Gee, if he was my dog," he said, "I'd sure let *you* pet him. I'd just say . . ."

"Well, he *ain't* your dog. An' he ain't *my* dog. He's my *man's* dog. And if he says no pettin', then there ain't gonna be no pettin'—and that's the whole size of it!"

Jud barely had time to kick himself for having forgotten all about the large-size jeans on the line before his eye caught a movement to his right. The dog had suddenly got to his feet, front legs straight, back ones in a semicrouch, one foot eight or ten inches ahead of the other. He was watching the woman with single-minded intensity, golden-brown eyes flicking now and then from her face to Jud's. Responding to the agitation in her voice, surely? Or expecting another signal—the signal that would . . .

It didn't bear thinking about. Time here for a little reassurance. "Don't you worry about me, ma'm, I won't touch him. Not even if he *is* the handsomest dog I ever saw, and the smartest too."

It worked—or something did—because her mood seemed to do an abrupt about-face and she smiled, a little wistfully. "Gee, I guess I can't be blamin' you, 'cause I'd sure admire to pet him myself, and play with him an' all that. Thing is—" She paused. A little conflict here, Jud thought, about whether to go ahead. He waited, trying to look interested but not too much so. Reaching a decision, she blurted out, "Thing is my man, he's gonna train this dog some more. Gonna make a *guard* dog out of him."

Once more Jud caught that note of childlike pride. "But I thought he was a guard dog already. He sure did act like one."

She shook her head impatiently. "Like I *tole* you, he's a *century* dog. Guard dog's different. Century just keeps on his toes and runs a person down an' *holds* 'em. Like Bo here done to you."

"Beau?"

"What I said—Bo. Short for Bojangles."

The name rang a bell but he couldn't place it until she added, "On account of Bo's black, like him, and sort of dances." Then he remembered seeing a fine tap dancer named Bill Robinson in an old movie. He was called "Bojangles of Harlem." It was a great name. "Your—uh—your man named him, I guess?"

She shook her head. "Already named when he got him."

Illogically, he was relieved to know that a man who could think up a name like that wasn't the same man who refused to let anybody pet his dog and also grew marijuana in the middle of one of the finest wilderness areas in the Northwest.

She returned now to her main subject. "Anyways, a guard dog's different from century. He don't mess around —just goes for yer throat."

Jud stared. "But—but that's just dogs they use in war, isn't it?"

She shook her head, impatient with his ignorance. "They use 'em for whatever they want really guarded. They're *killers*."

Jud couldn't believe that the relish with which she said "killers" originated with her. She was parroting. "My man" was the one who reveled in the idea of commanding a killer dog. Jud scanned the whole scene uneasily. If there'd been any doubt, there wasn't now: her man was a person to be avoided at any cost, and God knew where he might be at this moment. Jud told himself he'd be out of his mind to hang around chit-chatting with this strange child-woman.

So okay he was out of his mind; he couldn't stand not knowing just a little more. "That's real interesting, lady, and now I'd . . ."

She startled him with another giggle that belonged in the seventh grade. "Don't call me lady. Name's Yvonne. That's French." She pronounced it Yuh-von.

It just didn't seem right to correct her pronunciation of her own name. "Okay, Yv—uh—Yuhvon, what I was wondering was how your—er—man will go about turning Bo here into a guard dog."

"Well, Bull—ever'body calls him Bull 'cause his name's Durham. Get it—Bull Durham? Well, he studied up on it in a book." This she announced with unconcealed pride that never flagged as she proceeded to tell him all about it, quite unaware that she was telling a horror story. And Jud listened, appalled but unable to follow the impulse to flee back into the forest, to try to pretend this strange interlude at the edge of a pot grove was only a bad dream.

This Yvonne was frightening in her innocence, her utter ignorance of the difference between the monstrous and the ordinary.

What she chattered on about, as the sun hovered for a time above the jagged line of the ridge to the west, then dropped from sight, was the deliberate, calculated brutalization of an animal. An intelligent, playful, friendly dog was to be turned into a dangerous outlaw, fearing and hating every human creature except his master—and even the master could never be completely at ease with him.

Any details Yvonne neglected to mention Jud's imagination quickly supplied. It would begin with chaining the dog. A chain link or heavy wire enclosure would be better, but such a thing couldn't be built out here. Bull would be back some time the next morning. She let that cat out of the bag without noticing, and barely stopped short of revealing where he had gone. Wherever it was, he had gone there to recruit his old buddy Jacko, to help with the training process.

Jacko and Bull would be back together in the morning. If, that is—and she unbagged this cat in aggrieved tones— they didn't "get to drinkin'," in which case they might not show up until the following day.

During the time it took for Yvonne to get this far in her account of things to come, Bo had moved a step or two, yawned once, and stretched mightily, keeping an eye on the woman in case she might tell him not to do what he had in mind. Finding her preoccupied with her own words, he considered himself dismissed and trotted off to Jud's left. Jud performed contortions with his neck in an effort to keep both dog and woman in view at the same time. Bo moved directly toward the discarded backpack. Discarded how long ago? Ten minutes? Half an hour? The dog circled the pack, sniffing thoroughly. Dad's Unpatented Pemmican would no doubt smell ambrosial to him, adulterated though the scent might be by the sweat of a hiker's back. The thought would have prompted a grin if Jud hadn't been listening at the same time to a horror story. A few moments later, the catalog of fragrances completed, Bo trotted on and disappeared over the lip of the ravine. Tracking Jud in reverse, maybe? Funny to think that to the dog the Jud smell must reach for miles across the forest floor, clinging to the mosses, to the scratchy fingers of manzanita and salal, to the downsweeping branches of Port Orford cedar and Douglas fir.

But now Yvonne was getting to what she must consider —could it really be so?—the exciting part. "Jacko he's gonna be the bad guy, see? He's smaller than Bull, an' faster on his feet. He'll have this stick—kind of a pole— and step in and out—jab-jab-jab—an' holler an' cuss. And Bo he'll be on the chain. . . ."

Later—Jud tried not to hear about how many days the tormenting process might take—Bull would put Bo on a chain leash and walk him toward the spot where Jacko, wearing a padded outfit with a thick leather guard covering the right arm to the shoulder, was hidden. This would protect old Jacko from the teeth of his newly created enemy. He would leap from his ambush, yelling and threatening, whereupon Bo—unless he turned out to be one of the rare shepherds who would rather retreat than attack—would launch himself with a roar at his tormentor, ripping and slashing at the leather with the fearsome armament of his jaws until Bull dragged him away with the chain.

Later, Yvonne was explaining about what would come later when the unexpected happened. Jud had been standing there, arms at his sides, angry, and helpless, when from behind him a cold, wet, velvety muzzle was thrust into his left hand. Barely repressing a startled gasp, he felt the great head press against his thigh and looked down to see the dog's golden-brown eyes rolled ridiculously upward as if to gauge how his overture was going to be received. It didn't occur to him that a muzzle still dripping from a refreshing drink from the stream down in the ravine could be anything but welcome in the hand of this man-person.

He was right. It required a big effort on Jud's part to keep from dropping to his knees and flinging his arms around the neck and shoulder now pressed against him. But it wouldn't do. Though Yvonne hadn't noticed anything yet she would certainly notice a thing like that, and there was no guessing what her reaction might be. He had to content himself with surreptitiously sliding his hand along the muzzle to the cheek, pressing the head harder still against his leg, then up and over to rub thumb and fingers in the soft depressions behind the upthrust ears. The feel brought instant overpowering recollections of Bigfoot, who had always squirmed with delight at the same attentions. It could almost have *been* old Bigfoot, so familiar was the feel beneath his hand—except that Bigfoot's neck was thicker.

Yvonne had reached the point in her exposition at which Bull began loosing Bo from the chain to let him hurl himself on his enemy, then calling him off to begin the process over again.

"An' after that . . ." She broke off, peering at Jud with troubled eyes. "Well *hey!* How come you lookin' like you seen a creepy risin' up?"

Startled, Jud dragged his imagination back from where it had been. He hadn't the least idea what he'd been looking like, but surely the "creepy risin' up" look must have been caused by the thought of this dog turned into something that feared and hated and therefore was feared and hated in return. A creature that would kill.

But what could he say to this girl-woman with the troubled eyes? He floundered. "Gee, Yuhvon, it just seems—*you* know—*sad*—to make a dog mean when what he really feels is friendly."

Now it was her turn to look startled—but more than that. Jud didn't know any word for it. He was thinking fast, but with no experience to help him. "I mean, you could look at it this way. Take yourself—you're friendly. Would you like something to happen that made you mean and hurtful, so that folks'd be afraid of you?"

And it worked. She stared at him, eyes growing wider, more distressed. In the end she shook her head. "No—no, I purely *wouldn'* care for that. But . . . ain't nothin' I can *do* about . . ." She turned her troubled gaze to Bo and broke off abruptly. "Well *hey!*" More hurt than angry. "I tole you you wasn't s'posed to pet him. So how's come you *doin'* it?"

Not about to disclose it had been Bo's idea, he said, "Sorry, ma'm—Yuhvon, it was kind of an accident. He was just walking by and I reached out. . . ."

"Oh *sure*, you just reached out an' there he was. Well, it better not happen again. Anyway—" She looked this way and that, as if a little surprised to find herself here. She looked at the rifle the same way and lifted it. "Anyway, I got to go. Bull find out about me yakkin' away like this to a stranger he'd kick my butt for me. You better take off anyways, y'hear? Get on about yer business, and don't come back."

She sounded so dispirited that Jud tried to be comforting. "Well, I tell you, Yuhvon, I don't *feel* like a stranger. More like a friend."

A slight exaggeration, but not altogether. Either way, the result was magical. The shy smile that spread over her face was like a break in an overcast sky, and for that moment she was beautiful. "Well, *thank* you. Thank you *kinely*. That was—that was just purely a *sweet* thing to say!" Jud was profoundly grateful they were separated by a good eight or ten feet. Much closer and she might have kissed him. There must not, he thought, have been many nice things said to her in her lifetime.

All the same, it was time to get moving. "You're right," he said. "I better take off. I'd appreciate it if you'd point the way toward a road where maybe I could hitch a ride."

Now she shook her head a little, frowning. "It's a long ways, an' I never went out or come in on my own. Bull he always finds the way." She brightened a little, pointing. "But I do know we always head *that* way, an' Bull he says you keep a-goin' due east an' you'll make it."

Jud thanked her gravely, at the same time wondering why he'd asked. He had no intention of going any way but the way he'd come, and that was a lot more south than east. It didn't matter which route Bull would take. But then, you never knew when a scrap of information might come in handy.

"Well," he said, with the usual awkwardness of leave-taking, "it's been nice talking to you." He moved—stiffly because of having stood motionless for so long—to where his pack lay at the lip of the ravine. Kneeling, he tightened a strap here, a Velcro fastening there, in case something had worked loose when he'd thrown it off. Nothing had, but he went on fiddling with it, putting off the moment of departure. He wasn't going to see this dog again and it was more than a little like the sick emptiness he'd felt when he and Dad had taken old Bigfoot to the vet for the last time.

On an impulse he knew was pointless, illogical, he lifted

a flap and pulled out a sock, one he'd worn the day before and neglected to wash. Laying it on the ground, he put a foot on it and stood up, hoisting the pack to his shoulders with the familiar shrug. Maybe, before his new and dreadful life began, Bo would come across it and remember.

Yvonne was still standing there watching him. Now she waggled her fingers, little-girl style.

"So long," he said and threw one last look at the dog, who sat like an ebony carving, eyes following Jud's every move, big tongue lolling from the side of his jaw.

This was stupid. The longer Jud looked the more painful it got. And not altogether because of Bo. There was Yvonne, with her strange, unlikely appeal. She had been dealt a hand with few face-cards. She didn't deserve it. But there must be many like her. Thousands, likely. It was wrong. It was all wrong.

He smiled at her, feeling more than a little foolish, and waggled some fingers at her, so long as there was no one here to see. One more look at Bo, then he wheeled and plunged down the slope of the ravine. The wilderness was his refuge and friend. Or anyway it had been up to now.

CHAPTER

4

For perhaps thirty minutes Jud backtracked, concentrating on following the trail he had left for himself from the point at which he'd begun to follow the sound of Bo and his saucepan. Plenty of useless things occurred to him. Such as the notion of going home, somehow getting a rifle, hiking on back, and potting old Jacko and My Man Bull from ambush. Or going to the sheriff with a tip on how to make a big marijuana bust. Or bringing Dad back with him to—to what? To get himself shot. Good thinking! Then there was the really dandy one where he'd get his savings out of the bank and go *buy* Bo from Bull, who would for some reason refrain from shooting him on sight and who would furthermore be really hot to sell a trained shepherd for a hundred and twenty-seven bucks, give or take five.

There were plenty more useless ideas, some less idiotic than others but not by much. He had made it back to where his marked trail began. There he sat down on the same moss-grown boulder and sipped a few mouthfuls from his water bottle. It was getting low. He'd have to follow a little stream to its spring-fed source, and refill it. The lightning struck him in the middle of the final swallow and he choked, setting a squirrel to scolding in a fir tree high above.

Where had Bull gone to fetch old buddy Jacko? And how did he get there? So all right—if he did know the answers what difference would it make? The difference, dummy, was between doing something to save Bo and *not* doing something. Even if not to save him, to at least postpone the horrible procedure of turning him into something worse than a mad dog. Put a spoke in their wheel—slow them down—give them a bad time one way or another.

There was another question that he should have asked long since: How had this wilderness odd-couple managed to lug all that gear over maybe fifteen miles of rugged country to this place in the wilderness? The tent alone was of a size to daunt the strongest of men, and while this Bull was undoubtedly strong he wasn't Superman. And the lumber for the platform that kept the tent off wet ground: boards to cover an area of about twelve by fourteen feet, and two-by-fours to make a frame. Besides all that, to live there even during the dry months would require a lot of food, however spartan the diet, and Jud was aware almost to the ounce how much food a backpacker could carry, and how long he could keep going on it. Out here there could be no running to the supermarket for bacon and beans. Nearest supermarket must be twenty miles away, the nearest back-country store with gas pump probably half that distance.

Pack animals? Possible, but they were taboo in the wilderness. Too rough on the environment. Not that that would worry somebody like Bull. What would stop him was the absence of grazing areas out here. No, it almost had to be a wheeled vehicle and at least a primitive trail it could move on. This meant an old logging road. There were such roads in these mountains, a few of them even shown on the maps. There were still older trails hacked through the forests about a hundred years ago by miners of gold and silver to transport tools and machinery to their diggings. Surely a resourceful and persistent man could make use of such trails, providing he kept to a bare minimum any improvements on them and drove something with high clearance and four-wheel drive. Jeep maybe, or pickup with built-up suspension and extra-size tires.

He'd be taking a chance, of course, but according to Dad the forest service hadn't been able to do much patrolling since Vietnam days, when government economies cut into manpower. A man like Bull, Jud told himself, would have figured all these angles, along with plenty more, and balanced the risks against the rewards, the latter being big money in the sale of pot.

Further brow-furrowing told Jud that the jeep-or-whatever was undoubtedly kept hidden at some distance from the pot patch. If he'd been doing it he'd put a mile or two of untouched wilderness between the end of the trail and the camp. In the unlikely event that a hiker should stumble onto the vehicle, he could deduce where it had come from, but nothing more. The tent and other things could be packed to the campsite by men. Not easy, but possible.

Jud arrived at each new conclusion with mounting excitement. What was to be done with all these deductions he didn't know yet—but surely *something*. His first impulse was to study the map but he stopped himself abruptly. Hold it, dummy—first thing you've got to do is find out where you are! All he knew at the moment was where he was with relation to the marijuana grove, not with relation to the wilderness as a whole and where he'd started from. First sensible move was to climb to the top of a ridge where he could see far enough to get some kind of bearing.

One thing the Kalmiopsis had was plenty of ridges. Ridges that ran into other ridges or dropped off into canyons that ran into other canyons. Nothing followed any pattern, including the mountains. No east-west, north-south or any other identifiable drift. These were the roots of ancient mountains, with an eternity to prepare traps for the inattentive hiker, contriving even to mix up the vegetation along with the contours so that a person could wander from a mosquito-infested swamp to a forest dense with firs, from canyons thick with live oak to pine barrens breaking out with blisters of fiery red rock, and from there back into clutching thickets of manzanita. All this in the space of three or four hours even though each belonged to an altitude that should have been widely separated from any of the others. It was the kind of place, as Dad once put it, where "the water don't know, one day to the next, which way to run."

Thinking of ridges brought to mind the one back at the marijuana grove behind which the sun had gone down . . . how long ago? He looked at his watch. Must have been an hour by now. Well, one ridge was much like another if all you wanted to do was get up high and take a look around. On the other hand if his aim was to find the logging road, or whatever it was, it would make more sense to choose a ridge farther to the east. Most of the populated areas with such things as grocery stores lay in that direction. And if that *wasn't* his aim, what was?

The only objective that made real sense, of course, was

home. The quicker the better. Climb the nearest ridge to the south or east, orient himself, make camp, and take off as soon as it was light enough to move in the morning. Likely Dad would be home the day after, and the record would sure look better if he'd left Carla alone for only one night. Come to think of it, he hadn't given a thought to Carla and home since his ear had first caught the sound of Bo's saucepan game. As for the inner storm of resentment and guilt that had sent him careening out here in the first place, it seemed so far removed from him now that it might all have happened to somebody else.

Nothing was the same now, and all because a dog back there—a doomed dog—had said in the only way he knew how, "Hey, let's you and me be friends."

He had extracted one of his homemade granola bars from the pack and held it in his teeth while he shouldered the pack. Then he bit off a nourishing bite, gave his compass a glance, and set off, heading for whatever ridge lay to the northeast. In the morning he'd find the logging road, if it existed. And if he found it, what? He didn't know, but he had to do *something* or he wouldn't be able to stand himself.

He made it to the top of the ridge with no more than thirty or forty minutes of good visibility to spare. As he climbed—forcing himself for the last five hundred feet or so because he had covered many weary miles that day—dusk dogged his footsteps. Shadows deepened in the valleys below, and overhead a pale half-moon sailed up into a milky sky. Jud unslung his pack and dropped with it to the ground. His legs and lungs were telling him that enough was enough.

But there was still work to be done. Out came the precious map and the compass which he set on the rock beside him for ready reference. Reading topographical maps was never easy, with their scores of wavy lines representing variances in contour and elevation, and the dozens of watercourses, the larger ones with names, the others without. This time it was extra difficult because weariness tended to blur the lines, forcing him to squint and rub his eyes. The coordinating of map with visible features of the landscape all had to be done in his head. Fifteen minutes passed while he labored with eyes, map, and compass, but at the end he was satisfied that at last he knew where he was.

The highest eminence near at hand was Pearsoll Peak, rising to just over five thousand feet at the eastern boundary of the wilderness to the north and a little east of Jud's ridge. The stream he had crossed just before climbing the ridge had to be Crater Creek near its confluence with Granite Creek on the west. The map showed a primitive road (the classification between a dirt road and a trail) snaking its way westward just to the south of where he now sat and ending abruptly at a point which, if his calculations proved correct, lay almost exactly four and a half miles east of the marijuana grove. From there a wavering line on the map extended westward for a short distance. At first glance he missed it because it looked like one of the myriad contour lines, but a second look showed that it *crossed* several of those lines, followed one of them for about six hundred feet, then crossed some more. This had to mean that it was a trail or road even more primitive than the one so classified.

Straining his eyes to make sure he was seeing what he thought he was seeing, he followed the line a second time, telling himself sternly that he could be dead wrong. Still, he couldn't contain a growing excitement. This had to be what he was looking for. It was in the right place. The direction and distances all added up. And a line that crossed the contours had to represent man's work, not nature's.

With the nub of a pencil from the map case he drew a line from his present position to the point at which the primitive road ended and the all-but-invisible one began.

With the rewarding sense of having done a good day's work, he put away the compass and map, heaved himself up onto protesting legs, and shouldered the pack once more. At least it was all downhill from here to the campsite he'd spotted on the way up. Even more encouraging was the thought of the first hot food of the day.

It turned out to be an even better site than he'd made it out to be on his first quick look in passing. It was a small open space with all the comforts of home. An outcropping of rock at one side with a convenient shallow crevice in its top for a small fire. A tiny stream nearby that gurgled from the rocky wall of the ridge. A pair of young sumacs spaced just right to hold the nylon line over which he would throw his polyethylene tarp and make a tent of it. An unexpectedly abundant supply of fuel, thanks to a dead limb cast down by a winter storm from the only fir tree anywhere around—the same tree had shed a carpet of needles thick enough to scrape into the semblance of a mattress for his bedroll.

What more could he want? Well, maybe to be home with his feet under the table and Carla dishing up a batch of her spareribs and sauerkraut, or maybe her veal scallopini. She might be a pain in the neck, but he had to admit Carla knew her way around a kitchen. And come to think of it, it was Carla's special condensed beef-and-vegetable soup that would soon be warming, water added, in his little cookpot. Seasoned with all kinds of herbs and things, including plenty of salt to help rehydrate hikers who'd been sweating out body salts by the bucketful. Thoughts of the soup set his juices to flowing long before it was ready to eat and he hurried through his housekeeping chores at double speed.

When the soup was hot he forced himself to eat it a lot more slowly than he wanted to in order to savor it longer. Along with it he ate one of his packets of processed meat—ham in this case—and for dessert a two-ounce portion of home-dried apples, pears, and bananas, mixed. The only thing lacking was milk, but that was one item you couldn't carry with you. Powdered milk wouldn't do; he hate it.

He could easily have eaten the whole meal a second time, but one thing a backpacker could never afford was greed. Reluctantly he cleaned up and repacked everything but the cookpot, which he needed to heat water to wash his socks. One of Dad's rules was to wash each evening the light polyester ones worn next to the skin. The heavier wool-synthetic ones could make it for the duration of most hikes without washing. It was one of the outer ones he had left behind for Bo to smell and perhaps remember. Dumb thing to do, he told himself now. Perfectly good sock. But he wasn't sorry. Chances of it ever doing any good were about a million to one, especially since he had no idea *how* it would ever do any good. But so what—people won big bucks every day on lotteries against higher odds than that.

He washed the socks in warm soapy water, rinsed them in the stream, poured the wash water over the embers of the fire, and laid the socks on the heated rock to dry. After that it took only moments to strip to his shorts and slide into the waiting sleeping bag. Ah, the luxury! Often he stayed awake long enough to listen to the sounds of the night creatures all around—the rustlings, scurryings, and squeakings of the dwellers on the forest floor, the calls of the owls aloft, the sonar-squeak of bats, a sound almost too high for the human ear to detect. Tonight he had time only to recollect the feel of that furry wet muzzle thrust into his hand before he dropped into the abyss of sleep in which he heard nothing, knew nothing, and didn't even dream.

CHAPTER

5

He must have been thinking, if not dreaming, because when he came awake soon after dawn he knew what he was going to do. *Try* to do, anyway, against odds that hadn't got any better during the night.

He lay there for a minute, reveling in the warmth of the sleeping bag and putting off the shock that awaited him when he emerged into the chill of early spring in the mountains. At least the weather was on his side. What he could see of the sky was beautifully clear when it could as easily have been dripping rain. Well, maybe that was a good omen. He slowly drew his knees toward his chest, tensed, and exploded out of his warm nest like a chukar flushed from cover. War-dancing his way into his clothes, then more sedately putting his boots on, he dashed to the stream and scooped icewater over his face.

Breakfast was cold too, but no matter; he was driven now by a sense of urgency that robbed of all significance such things as hot food and leisurely preparations for departure. If he didn't arrive at what he hoped—and also feared—would be a rendezvous with Bull and old buddy Jacko, there'd be no use going at all. And there'd be no use going under any circumstances if even one of his calculations—which were two-thirds guesswork—was wrong. But as Dad was given to saying, "If you don't draw the card you want, go with what you've got!"

And Jud went. The last thing he did was to empty a bottle of water on his impromptu fireplace, stirring the already cold ashes with a stick, refilling the bottle and restoring it to its proper compartment before setting the pack on his back.

Near and far the birds were calling now. It was nesting season and they had a lot to talk about, and since there is no cheerier sound in creation, Jud's spirits rose as he swung along, keeping an eye on what lay ahead, following the contours, following stream beds when handy, veering off course now and then to take advantage of level, nearly open spaces (of which there were always more in the mountains than one would believe from a distance), and following also his compass course, about ten points west of north. Following last of all the sort of built-in radar signal that most veteran hikers recognize—and trust, but only up to a certain point, that point being the one at which you said hold on now, might be wrong. Confidence was the key; when that faltered, check the compass. Check the map. Check everything.

The miles went by and the sun rose higher. Jud got rid of his anorak without slackening his pace, and before he was ready for it his watch said eight o'clock and his map said any time now you'll see the old logging road branching off to the left. About five hundred yards farther along, it did, angling across the side of another of those endless ridges, heading for its crest. He slowed his pace and bent to search the ground for signs that anything on wheels had passed that way.

There were no tracks of any sort, or if there were he couldn't make them out. To be sure, this road—if you could stretch your imagination enough to call it that—was mostly over rock. It would take an army tank to make tracks on it. But this wasn't the time to give up and he went on, following that uncertain line on the map that told him this was indeed, or once had been, a passable road—at least for horse-drawn vehicles. It followed the peak of the ridge for about a hundred feet, then headed downward on the easy slope to the north. Soon he found himself among trees again—mountain hemlock they were, with flowering plants he didn't recognize growing at their feet. Soon the slope leveled off and a sparsely wooded forest of fir lay before him. Here for the first time he spied where the heavy hand of man had been at work.

In among the trees, often masked by the undergrowth around them, were the stumps of bigger trees. Giant first-growth firs. This area had been logged over, maybe sixty years ago, judging from the size of the second-growth trees towering among them.

Jud took all this in with a sweeping glance, but what caught his eye and held it was a smaller stump cut level with the ground unlike the old ones whose stumps stood as high as six or seven feet. Quickly he spotted a second small stump, and soon a third, at intervals of about forty feet. The cuts showed grayish-white against the green and somber brown of the rest of the forest. Felled fairly recently, the trees lay where they had fallen, limbs blackened and bare of needles. No question now: they had been cut in order to open again what had been a passable road long ago. No doubt others beyond these had been cut as well.

Even while he felt welling up inside him the exultation of having been right on almost every point, a sort of primordial wariness took hold and he halted in midstride, ears straining to hear distant sounds, eyes probing the forest ahead and on either side. If he was so all-fired smart and right about everything, he was now in enemy country and had better not forget it. There was no movement though but that of birds, no sounds but theirs, and in a few moments he moved on.

Through the trees the trail was plain, thanks to the occasional felled tree. Even so he scanned the ground as he walked, looking for signs that something with wheels had passed—a crushed patch of moss maybe, or a track in the carpet of needles. Because he was looking down he nearly missed the most obvious of signs. Beside the trail an insignificant larch sapling had grown at a slant, stealing a little sunlight from an encroaching fir, and now Jud's attention was suddenly captured by a glimpse of raw heartwood. A limb of the sapling had broken just at eye level and was hanging by a shred of bark. Jud examined the break, felt it, smelled it. No question, the break was new. Not a clear break but twisted as if it had been caught by something both unyielding and in motion. Its leaves had been stripped from it and lay now in a small scattering five or six feet from the tree in the direction from which Jud had come. This had to mean the pickup-or-whatever had been moving eastward, away from, not toward, the pot plantation.

So he was in time. Plenty of time, more than likely, and then some. Bull had passed here in his vehicle at least a day or two ago on the way to wherever old Jacko was waiting. Yvonne had said only that they'd be back in the morning and it was all but impossible they could have passed this point already unless they had started long before daylight. Jud himself had started before full daylight, and it was only eight-twenty now. He just couldn't see that pair as early risers, especially if they'd got to drinking the night before. And if that was what happened and they weren't to come until the following morning, the jig was up for Jud anyway. He couldn't possibly spend another twenty-four hours out here, plus the eight or so it would take him to get home. He'd packed food for a day and a night, with a little left to get home on; there was no way he could make it last. One thing a hiker could never afford to do was go very long without eating. Deprivation meant fatigue and fatigue meant missteps resulting in injury and miscalculations, resulting in going off course, walking in circles, and maybe—in the end—panic.

As it was, he could hang around here until noon or two p.m. at the outside. And even if he'd had twice the amount of rations, a second night away from home was out of the question. He'd be lucky to get Dad to forgive *one* night. But two? Forget it.

For half a minute he stood listening. All the sounds he heard were wilderness sounds but one. That was the hum of an aircraft so far off that his ear nearly missed it, and soon it died away. Satisfied that no vehicle was anywhere within miles, he shucked off the pack and sat down with his back against the rough bark of a fir. Time to check the map again.

A careful study showed that this ghost of a road ended at the foot of the second ridge due west of where he sat, a distance of three miles or more. An hour without pushing it. Maybe half an hour most other places—but that's the way it was in the Kal. He put the map case away and treated himself to half a bar of pemmican and a swig of water. After that he sat and enjoyed the breezes that were all there was left of what had no doubt been a stiff onshore wind along the California beaches to the southwest.

But he couldn't enjoy them long before thoughts of what still lay ahead intruded, taking all the fun out of resting. Within five minutes he was on his way again.

His calculation of the time was off by a mere fifteen minutes. When he arrived at what had to be the end of the road it was nearly nine-thirty. It had to be the end because the ridge looming dead ahead met another ridge trending at a right angle to it. Dead end. Nothing on wheels could go farther. Furthermore, a strange rock formation at the angle where the two ridges met formed a huge overhang from the lip of which grew masses of poison oak, menacing but beautiful in its springtime garb of glistening green. Some of it was climbing on the ledge above, but more was trailing down to form a perfect hiding place, even for objects as big as a small truck or car. This luxuriant curtain's longer tendrils hung three or four feet above the ground, so those susceptible to the poison could duck under them in safety. Already safe, Jud parted them and stepped into the gloomy cavern behind.

First thing to be seen was the dark gleam of water trickling down the wall of rock to form a shallow pool. Not a true spring, it was surface water still slowly draining the ridge above after the last fall of rain. Once his eyes got used to the gloom he could see that the floor of the place was wet where the pool had receded. Scooping up a handful of earth, he found it was composed of gritty mud. There is no better substance to retain prints left by human or wheel, and in only a few moments he found both. No great tracking skill was needed to know that a man with boots about four sizes larger than Jud's had come in and something with wide tires had gone out.

He'd been right all the way. Batting a thousand! The feeling of triumph didn't last long. From here on, more than likely, his batting average would plunge. Now everything was up for grabs. He couldn't see any farther than the end of his nose, and there was no map to help him out.

First thing to do was to back out on hands and knees, smoothing the mud over his own tracks as he went. Probably Bull and company wouldn't even notice them, but it would be foolhardy to take a chance. Next thing was to find himself a hiding place from which he could see both the cave and the last fifty yards or so of the trail down which he had come.

It wasn't easy. Perching in a tree limb for however long it might take was out of the question. He'd already been up a tree with a gun pointed at him and was in no hurry for a repeat. In case he had to run for it, the ground was the place to be. He'd bet on himself to elude almost anybody in the wilderness. Considering and rejecting several possibilities, he settled on a spot behind a boat-shaped boulder twenty feet up the side of the northeastward-trending ridge. There was room to lie down behind it and enough moss and other low ground cover to make it comfortable. Experimenting, he found he needed to expose his head only as far as the eyes to see the cave, and just a bit farther to see the trail as it made its rocky way along the foot of the opposing ridge.

Now came the hard part—waiting. Seated next to the boulder, he spent a while redistributing items in his pack to shift its weight up a little higher. The center of gravity tended to change as the edibles were consumed, and a good balance could make a difference in the ease of carrying it. That done, he considered stashing the pack somewhere beyond sight of this spot, in case he needed to skin out in a hurry—but in the end he ruled it out. The direction of a dash for safety was something he couldn't predict.

Having got that far, he couldn't avoid dwelling for a while on his approaching encounter with two men who would probably consider him a bug that needed stepping on. An uncomfortable line of thought, and useless besides, so he made an effort to think about something else. In this he had the help of a pair of brown lizards with bright blue eyes that suddenly darted around the curve of his boulder, one in pursuit of the other. They proceeded to put on a show that was good for several minutes of nonthinking. Changing roles—pursuer and pursued—they zipped up, down, and to all sides, stopping at intervals on whatever would be a dime to a lizard. During the stops they appeared to be staring with bulging eyes at nothing whatsoever, least of all each other, then off they would go again. Some sort of mating game, Jud supposed. It didn't seem to be getting anywhere though, and ended in a flash of movement when he lifted a hand to scratch an itch.

Next he heard the discordant call of a crow high overhead, followed by a chorus of its friends and relatives and a glimpse of the black marauders where a broad patch of sky was visible between fringes of tree cover. Even crows were a pleasure to watch, and he leaned back, using his pack for a pillow. Might even be some hawks along for variety.

Of course the inevitable happened, and for more than an hour he didn't have to think about anything because his thoughts took the form of dreams in which all sorts of things happened but none made any sense. Plenty made sense, though, when his eyes flipped open and he sat up galvanically. The sound was far away but could be mistaken for nothing other than what it was: a vehicle laboring over rough ground in one of its lower gears.

Jud's instinct was to fling himself into his hiding place behind the boulder, dragging the backpack with him. He forced himself to ignore it. No need to get in a sweat. He stood up, the better to see and hear. Nothing to see yet, of

course, nor would there be for a while. Plenty of time—
just keep your cool. At a guess the vehicle was at least
two miles away, and probably making about three miles an
hour. All the same he found himself moistening dry lips
and swallowing air, simultaneously thinking of all the hun-
dreds of places he'd rather be than here. Just being here
must mean he'd lost his marbles. He was about as well
equipped to pull off this caper as Little Bo-Peep, and if he
had a grain of sense left he'd use it to head down into the
next canyon and keep on going.

What he did instead was to place his pack where it would
stick out just a few inches beyond the boulder. He then
descended in a series of leaps to the level of the cave, where
he looked back up. He could see the end of the pack all
right but not readily, and only because he knew it was
there. Besides, what reason would they have for looking
up there?

But there was something else . . . Damn! His hair! It
wasn't as yellow as it used to be, but still it would stand out
against the greens and browns of the ridge like a candle in
a coal mine. He did a mountain-goat act back to his boulder
and groped in a pocket of the pack, extracting his hat. A
shapeless object made of water-repellent camouflage cloth,
it had just enough brim to keep the rain out of his eyes—
or in this case to cover his hair. He jammed it on his head
and stood listening again. The sound was still audible, but
fainter now. That could mean it had been atop a ridge
before and had descended behind another, or that it had
reached one of the relatively smooth stretches and gone up
to third gear maybe. There were a few such places—the fir
grove one of them.

He pulled the pack back out of sight and lay down in
its place, peering from underneath the hat brim. It was
maybe sixty feet from the rock overhang, which was plain

enough to see, but he wished he could see in under it better. What they did when they put the car in there would make all the difference.

Unable to stay still, he jumped up, went back to the front of the cave, and checked the ground once more for traces of his having been there. Back up to his rock again, he stood making a mental inventory of ways to get away from there fast if they should spot him. Not that he was really worried, but you had to be ready for the unexpected. At least he'd have a good headstart, be off and running while they scrambled up the side of the ridge.

Suddenly the distant engine's whine was not so distant anymore and he whirled, every sense alert. Nothing to be seen yet, but he dropped down behind the rock and wriggled forward, tugging the hat low over his eyes. Again the sound level dropped, but not as far and not for as long as before. He lay with eyes riveted to the line of scrub pines at the peak of the next ridge over. He was taking air in short gulps, as if the oxygen were thinning out. Still the noise rose and fell, whined and hummed and groaned and complained, but nothing appeared in view. It was like one of those movie-sound sequences when Something Evil was coming nearer—nearer . . . Kettledrums—thousands of voices chanting—hoofbeats—elephants trumpeting—captives moaning. . . .

Just when Jud thought he couldn't stand it another moment, but with nothing to do if he couldn't, there it came— a high-slung dirty-gray pickup, pitching and bouncing like some demented amusement-park ride, making the most of its high-suspension and outsized tires, bulling its way over impossible ground. It wasn't old but had lived a life that aged it fast. To be inside it, Jud thought, must be like taking Niagara Falls in a barrel. So much the better; when they got out they'd probably have a hard time telling up from down, let alone north from south—or what lay behind a boulder twenty feet above their heads.

The truck rocked and bucketed down the slope to the level stretch that led to the curtain of poison oak. While it was still moving, the passenger door opened and a man swung down, and as it came to a halt he reached into its bed and hefted out two dirty canvas bags lumpy with their contents, and set them off to one side. They looked heavy but the man handled them as easily as if they'd been stuffed with cotton. No wonder. Wearing boots, combat fatigue pants, and a shirt with sleeves cut off at the shoulder seams, he looked powerful enough to lift the truck itself. A large tattoo adorned his upper arm. He wore a black beard, straggling hair to match, and his great beak of a nose surely must have been broken more than once. He was about thirty years old. When Jud picked a man to make an enemy of, Jud told himself sardonically, he picked the best. There could be little doubt that this was Bull. In spite of the tension of the moment, Jud's mind went off on a sidetrack, speculating about what strange quirk of fate had brought the childlike Yvonne and this man together, and kept them so. His appearance readily bore out what she had said, or anyway implied—that there was little kindness in him, or tenderness, or any of the other things that were regarded as drawing men and women together. None of this would he ever have thought of if it hadn't been for the unexpected appealing quality of Yvonne.

Once the bags were out of the way, the man called to the driver above the sound of the idling engine. "Okay— turn 'er around!"

"Right!" The owner of the second voice, obviously old buddy Jacko, was on the wrong side for Jud to get a look at him, but he didn't mind waiting a while for the pleasure.

Followed then a series of hand signals and commands by

the big man. "Straight back—little more—little more—hold it! Now sharp right. Easy—easy—hold 'er there."

"Gotcha!"

About two minutes of this, then the pickup backed under the vine curtain, whose longest tendrils swept the cab as it passed under and dropped into place again. Now all Jud could see, dimly, was one headlight and part of the bumper. Bull followed the truck in. The men spoke briefly but the words were muffled. Jud strained his ears but heard no other sounds. That was encouraging—or anyway a little.

He tensed. They were coming out. Now he'd know for sure. Jacko was first to crawl from under the vines. Even before he got to his feet, Jud saw that his hands were empty and breathed a trifle easier. Once erect, Jacko bore a startling resemblance to a bear on its hind legs. Short, bowed legs in brown canvas-looking pants supported a torso shaped like an oil drum—thick, heavy, running to paunch but still powerful, and skimpily covered by a dark green undershirt. He was the hairiest man Jud had ever seen. Hair sprouted from nearly every visible inch of skin, including arms and shoulders, but not his head, which was as bald as a soccer ball and about the same shape. He was clean-shaven, or had been about twelve hours ago. The surprising thing was the face. All the rest of him conveyed the impression of brutish power, but his expression was of unassailable good will, as if the whole world was his friend. Everybody's old buddy Jacko. Jud absorbed these impressions in the few seconds before Bull emerged to stand beside his friend. In his hand was a bottle, which he flourished, winking exaggeratedly. "Little snort to get me back to mama." He tipped it back, then handed it to Jacko. "Finish 'er off, then go put it back in the truck."

Jud watched this exchange with relief. Bottles didn't matter; what he'd been fearing to see Bull holding was a distributor head, a handful of sparkplugs, anything without which the pickup wouldn't run. It wouldn't do to have these guys stealing his thunder. But apparently Bull had good reason to feel sure nobody would discover the hiding place.

As Jacko started back with the bottle, Bull said, "Sure you don't touch them vines. And comin' back be sure you cover any marks you see—tracks—whatever."

While the other complied, Bull stood looking idly around, and that was the moment chosen by fate in the form of a lizard to scuttle from nowhere and dash the length of Jud's bare forearm. In only an instant he realized what it was, but so violently had he suppressed a startled yip that contracting his chest muscles caused a twitch of movement that shouldn't even have been noticed. The bearded man caught it, though, from the corner of an eye, and turned his head suddenly, scanning the ridge above him.

Jud had time to do nothing but shut his eyes in case their whites might be visible. He didn't breathe. In a moment his eyes refused to stay shut, opening to a beetle-browed squint in time to see Jacko back out from under the vines, making sweeping movements with his hands. Undistracted, Bull went on with his visual sweep of the ridge.

"What's up, doc?" Jacko's gravelly voice, muted.

No reply. Jud felt his nerves tighten like fiddle strings. Then, mercifully, "Critter up there. Squirrel, rabbit maybe." He turned. "Okay, let's hit the trail." He swung one of the bags over a shoulder.

His companion eyed the second bag with exaggerated distaste. "Ah, hell with it. Le's go back to town. Drink a little beer, shoot a little pool . . ."

"Laugh a minute, that's you, ol' buddy. C'mon, get your rear in gear."

Grinning like the jack-o-lantern for which Jud thought he might have been nicknamed, Jacko hoisted the other bag. "Lead on, big Daddy."

Jud cautiously took his first real breath in minutes, but he didn't stir until the pair had moved well off to the left, following the base of the north-trending ridge. Only when they passed from view did he get to his feet, stretching cramped legs and arms and peering toward the spot where his prey had vanished.

Time to get his little surprise party under way. He slung his pack over one shoulder. Wouldn't be lugging it for long. Then he set off to dog the footsteps of those who would probably become his bitter enemies.

CHAPTER
6

Dodging from one cover to another in case the men might glance back, Jud followed them just long enough to make sure they were on a course as close to due west as the terrain would allow, then veered off to the left. About a hundred feet in that direction he found what he was looking for, a temporary hiding place for the pack. A deep crevice in a buckskin boulder of a particularly vivid gray-green. Easy to find again. Then, moving swiftly without the encumbering pack, he retraced the route back to the pickup.

It was the work of about three minutes to open the hood, remove the air filter from the carburetor, and with the screwdriver blade of his knife to pry out the little flutter valve that controls the flow of air into the mechanism. Then he replaced the filter, concealing his exercise in sabotage. The longer it took them to find the trouble the madder they'd be.

What it would mean, once they'd discovered his handiwork, would be that one or both of them would have sooner or later to make the long hike to a town big enough to have a garage with a good stock of parts and then hike all the way back to make the repair. It couldn't possibly take less than two days, and more likely three.

So far so good, but Jud wasn't through yet. Now for the dangerous part. His watch told him thirteen minutes had passed since the men had left this hiding place. Surely they couldn't have gone too far, and sounds carried a long way out here. He stepped to the door on the driver's side, and pulled it open. Then he took a deep breath and mashed the heel of his hand down on the horn button.

As car horns went, this one was no great shakes—not a patch on the power-driven bellow of Dad's sixteen-wheeler —but here in these mountain fastnesses it blared out like the trumpet of doom. He held it for several seconds so that there could be no missing it, then tapped out a derisive ta-ta-ta-da-da by way of saying, "Hey, creeps, how do you like *them* apples?" After laying a false trail in the soft earth, he bounded like an antelope up the side of the ridge to a point on top of the rocky ledge from the lip of which grew the poison oak curtain, and lay down on his belly to wait. And to watch. It was a harebrained thing to do when he could have been swiftly putting a lot of distance between himself and this place, but having gone to all this trouble he couldn't bear to miss the fun.

He could hear them long before they came into view. Two pairs of boots propelling heavy bodies over rough ground at a speed they were ill conditioned for. Then, as the distance narrowed, grunts, tortured breathing, occasional explosive curses as missteps made them stumble. A few minutes of this, growing louder, nearer, and they lurched into view below and to the right of Jud's lofty perch. Bull appeared first, his thick arms pumping, glistening with sweat, beard bisected by the agonized grin of a man reaching the limit of his endurance. Behind by a few staggering paces came Jacko in a similar state, chest and belly heaving like shoaling waves, bald head turning red as a sunset. Fascinated, Jud flicked his gaze from one to the other. This beat anything he'd ever watched on television. They swayed to a halt in front of the evil curtain, fighting for air and more air. First to achieve speech was Jacko, whose words, interspersed with gasps and unintelligible to Jud, brought an impatient shake of Bull's head and a pointing gesture to the ground in front of them, and a single word: "Tracks!"

Ha! The unseen onlooker didn't say the word, but it was loud and clear in his head. His strategy was paying off. He'd taken pains to make a clear set of tracks that led out from under the curtain and continued in an easterly direction, stopping when they reached a rock slab. Jud had then made a wide U-turn, leaping from rock to rock to the point at which he'd started up the ridge.

Now came the payoff. Bull crouched, ducked under the vines, followed in a moment by his friend. Now Jud could see no more of them, and he stopped breathing, the better to miss no sound. For a long interval there was nothing to hear but he could easily imagine what was going on. First they would stare at the pickup. Its hood was up, its door open—not the way they'd left it. Now his ear caught muffled vocal rumblings. Then nothing for a while. Then more rumblings followed by a sound that was music to the avid listener's ears. The pulsating whine-whirr of a starter that wasn't starting anything. Pause. Same thing again. Rumble-rumble—this time a little louder. Tempers wearing a little thin down there? More nonstarting starter noises. *Loud* rumble.

Now protracted silence. They were checking everything —ignition wires, sparkplug terminals, distributor cap, battery cables, everything they could think of. No telling how long before they got around to the carburetor. And all this time Jud could have been doing the smart thing, getting the hell-and-gone out of there, getting on with the next item on the agenda. Lord knew there was still plenty to do, and even if there wasn't it was dumb to make himself a sitting duck; sooner or later they'd come looking for him with blood in their eyes.

Still he couldn't bring himself to do the smart thing. Any minute now the fireworks would go off and he couldn't miss *that*. Time enough then to do the disappearing act.

Then it happened. A great rolling barrage, almost wholly audible, of the strongest, foulest, most explosive words available in the English language—mostly in Bull's harsh voice. Jud had heard all the words before, at one time or another, but never all at once and in such various and artistic combinations. Grinning blissfully, he waited until Bull ran out of words at last, then rolled over twice to get well below the rim of rock, and started down the westward slope of the ridge. Objective number one: two canvas sacks unceremoniously dumped somewhere along the trail ahead.

From the moment he'd seen them slung over the men's backs nearly half an hour ago, those sacks had become an important part of his plot, adding a whole new dimension to it. They could hardly contain anything but supplies, mostly food, and their size and bulk seemed to indicate they must contain enough to keep three people going for a week or more. Deprived of them, somebody would have to hike out for more, a lot sooner than later. The car repair could be put off for a while, but not this.

Finding the sacks was ridiculously easy. Jud didn't pretend to be an expert tracker, but this route had been used so many times that only a newcomer to hiking could miss the signs. Patches of ground cover crushed more than once and struggling to grow; pebbles kicked to either side of a pebble-free line that snaked along, dodging barriers but generally heading due west; even slashes made, probably with a machete, where brush intruded on the path of least resistance.

The bags were lying no more than six feet apart in the middle of a ragged grove of madrones that grew from undergrowth comprised mainly of hazel brush and poison oak, the latter plainly showing that the machete had been along that way. The setting could hardly have been better suited to his purpose. After a quick glance inside one of the bags assured him it did indeed contain food in cans, boxes, and jars, he slung it over his shoulder, where it felt as unwieldy as a corpse, and staggered up the slope on the left to the thickest patch of poison oak in sight. There he stuffed the sack in, under, and between the vines, then artfully arranged them to cover it completely. Stepping back he eyed his handiwork critically and was satisfied. He couldn't see the bag himself, so how could anyone else?

Now he hurried back to the other bag. Keeping an ear cocked for the sounds of voices or of men on the move, he rummaged in the bag and extracted a can of corned beef hash and another of sardines. Not a combination you'd find on the menu at the Ritz maybe, but his mouth watered anyway. The sardine can fit neatly into a hip pocket, the hash would ride not too uncomfortably stuffed inside his shirt. It would do until he got back to where he'd left his pack.

It was a temptation to wait around to see the fun when his burly friends discovered that The Shadow had struck again, but his luck had held this far—no sense in crowding it. This time they'd be on the lookout for him. Anyway, he'd heard all the obscenities once already today; no use running through the list again. He hid the second sack not far from the first, picked out a landmark—a madrone that for reasons of its own had grown in a long curved arc completely bare of leaves or branches until both appeared in a sort of tuft like a palm tree's high above the ground—then quickly headed back toward where the pack lay hidden.

He had just located it, found space in it to stow the cans, and got a fair start on the way to the next phase of Operation Sabotage when he heard—faint but unmistakable—the roar of rage that could have come from no source but the persecuted and bedeviled Bull. He and Jacko had no doubt been looking for the sacks for a while, thinking they'd picked the wrong places to look, but had now discovered the bitter truth: their provisions were gone, lost, stolen, spirited away. There was a fiend loose in the wilderness and he—it—was out to do them in.

The fiend's moment of triumph lasted only until a disturbing thought assailed him. What if Bull would go and fetch Bo to sniff out the sacks? But how would the dog know what he was supposed to find? He wouldn't know what the sacks smelled like. At that point a truly appalling thought occurred to him: maybe Bo couldn't know what the sacks smelled like, but he'd certainly know the scent of Jud!

It was a scary thought but he put his mind to work on the possibilities. In the first place, a shepherd wasn't a natural tracker, like a bloodhound; he had to be trained. Nothing Yvonne had said indicated Bo's training went beyond what was needed for sentry duty. In any case Jud was willing to take his chances that the dog wouldn't harm him if he did find him. More likely the two of them would have a joyful, tail-wagging reunion. And after that . . . Jud knew perfectly well what might happen after that, but he hadn't wanted to admit it. What he'd do if Bo found him would be to take off with the dog right behind him, and get as far away from here as possible before nightfall. The long and short of it was he'd *steal* him. Steal was a harsh word and he'd been shying away from it while knowing all along that's what he'd do if he got the chance. And nothing would ever convince him it was wrong—not in this case. An uneasy thought poked at the back of his mind: Dad might not see it that way. Might even make him report the theft, *and* the pot farm, to the sheriff's office. But that was something to worry about later.

Anyway, this last notion was a pipedream, wishful thinking. How could he hang around here for the hour or so it would take the men to get Bo and bring him back here? And if they did, how did he know they'd turn Bo loose to find him instead of keeping him on a leash and coming right along with him? Some tail-wagging reunion!

No, the only sensible thing to do now was to follow the course he'd planned earlier, and the sooner the better. The plan would take him on a wide detour to the south and around to the west of the pot patch. West was where he wanted to be, because the prevailing winds blew from west-southwest and he had good use for this evening's breezes.

The breezes involved an altogether new development in his plot-as-you-go procedure. It was a facet of the plan that was either totally brilliant or the dumbest idea that had ever entered his head—and probably suicidal into the bargain. It was so unlikely to succeed that he tried to pretend he really was just going to kick it around, not actually follow through with it at all. It had sprung into his head almost immediately after the thought of hiding the sacks.

Originally, when he spotted the sacks, the idea had been simply to deprive Bull of their use, making things even more difficult for him, then to head for home while there were still enough daylight hours ahead. There was no other choice—his pack held barely enough food as it was.

Food. That did it. There was probably enough food in those bags to keep him going for a month. But what did he plan to *do* with an extra night out here? He knew the answer to that, but he couldn't afford to admit it; it was too far-fetched, unrealistic, impossible. Better to see it for what it was: one of those daydreams a person was always having. Getting rich and famous, by means unspecified. That sort of thing.

The trouble was that only a few minutes ago he'd taken the first small step out onto the high diving board. Those two cans of food said plainly: you're going to try it! But that was only the first step; it was a long way to the end of the board. To be honest, he had taken another step: the very fact that he was heading west this minute, instead of southeast. So what? He could go to the pot patch, have a look and a listen, maybe learn something useful, and still make it home before dark. Well, maybe not quite—but not long after; this time of year it didn't get really dark until nearly ten o'clock.

But what could he learn that he didn't know already? Probably nothing. And every step in that direction would put him farther from home. Face it, to go home was the only thing that made sense. The other would be like taking off from a high cliff with a set of homemade wings. And *why* would he be doing it? Because now he had a can of sardines that he didn't have before. Good thinking!

He slowed, stopped. There was a handy rock nearby. It would make sense to take a short break. A little snack, a little drink. Sitting, sipping, snacking, he took a fresh look at the pros and cons of heading south. No contest. Like the National League versus the Little League. In the first place, he'd been in trouble—bad trouble—before he'd even left home, and every minute since then was only making things worse. Even if he hadn't left home at all, he'd still have to face Dad and tell him about blowing his cool and making lumps on Mattingly. Another promise broken. And *then* he'd have to tell Dad he'd blamed the whole mess on *him* for not getting home for the birthday, and from there gone crashing off into the wilderness to show what he thought of him, and Carla too.

And after *that*, if he followed the plan he wasn't admitting even existed and stayed away another night, he'd have the added fun of telling Dad his boy Judson had been stupid enough, just plain *dumb* enough to . . . to . . . to steal, entice, or otherwise take away a valuable dog from the man who owned him because the man wanted to make a guard dog out of him. What a plot! Dad would love it. Probably double his allowance and apologize for having thought harsh thoughts about him.

Having come to the only conclusion possible to him, Jud swallowed his last morsel of granola bar and headed west. Maybe he'd get lucky and Bull Durham would beat his brains out and he wouldn't have to tell Dad anything.

CHAPTER

7

Methodically working his way along a wide southward loop around the pot farm, Jud moved warily, silently, avoiding what few level open spaces there were. He was in hostile country now and being actively hunted, for all he knew, so it would be foolhardy to take chances until he had to. The time for taking chances—big ones—would come soon enough.

Progress was slower this way but he was in no hurry; his aim was to give Bull and Jacko time to let their rage cool, to have a meal, make plans about what to do next. They might work on another bottle, or smoke some home-grown pot and get mellow enough to give no thought to their tormentor. And they might not. Jud improved his time by trying to think what he would do in Bull's place.

For one thing he might start trying to be a little more decent to poor Yvonne, who already had the cards stacked against her. Though what did he know about it? The big slob seemed to suit her all right. All of which was beside the point. If he were Bull, and not under the influence of anything stronger than horse sense, he'd keep his eyes and ears open for anything out of the ordinary, such as the behavior of the jays and squirrels, both of whom were quick to sound off when strangers came sneaking around. Also, he'd watch Bo, whose nose and ears were likely to signal things undetected by human senses. More than that, he'd send Bo out on sentry duty. If the dog returned without giving an alarm, he'd send him out again later on. And finally, just before dark, he'd take a turn around himself, rifle in hand.

Maybe Bull wouldn't do all—or even any—of these things, but the smart thing for Jud was to assume that he would and behave accordingly. One thing almost had to be certain: that Bull would send Bo out at least once. That, after all, was what the dog was *for*—and this brought Jud smack up against the unyielding, inescapable fact that he'd been doing his best all day to forget. The fact that he was about to risk everything—his safety, maybe even his life—on a roll of the dice. Worse than that: he was playing Russian roulette with a six-shooter loaded with *five* bullets, not one.

What did he really know about trained dogs? Next to nothing. Logic and common sense told him that such a dog, commanded by his master to do what he was trained to do, would do it, regardless of who the victim was. What made him think that *he* would be an exception? No reason— wishful thinking—stupid optimism.

Stupid or not, it was all he had and he wasn't going to back out now. If you don't draw the card you want, go with what you've got. On the other hand, what if you didn't have much to begin with? Well, that was it: all Dad's fault. His mouth twitched in a way that felt like a grin. He paused for another look at the map and then moved on.

The sun had sunk behind the jumble of mountain ridges to the west by the time he judged himself to be at his destination or near enough so that a little reconnoitering was in order. Just ahead was a stand of surprisingly huge western hemlock, some with trunks maybe ten feet in diameter. Their tops, far overhead, were still touched with the light of the sinking sun, and from the bottom of the slope below him came the gurgle of swift-moving water. One of the Chetco's many tributary creeks, a fair-size one by the sound of it.

Stashing his pack on the shady side of the only white rock in sight, he set off to find how close he had come to his objective. The creek flowed westward here and he followed its east-trending gully until it veered sharply south at the base of a steep though not high ridge. This he climbed, choosing footholds with great care, not only because to fall would be disastrous but also because a stone dislodged here would make enough noise to cause another kind of disaster. He needn't have worried. The ridge wasn't a ridge at all but the edge of a plateau. Plenty of fir trees, plenty of brush beneath them, but not a hemlock to be seen. The Kalmiopsis was playing her usual tricks, and he'd missed his goal by . . . by about half a mile, as it turned out.

It was thirty minutes before he found the clearing with its marijuana crop, and the tent was at the wrong end of it. He dropped to the ground in the lee of a windfall fir while he figured it all out. He'd proceeded northward from the spot at which he should have headed east. Not really a bad miscalculation, but a nuisance. Now he'd have to toil all the way back to his pack. On the other hand this had brought him to a point on the perimeter of the clearing that was closer to the tent. He could hear and see better—that is, he could once he'd eased a little farther up the slope on which he now lay.

First he rolled onto his back, peering up at the tops of the firs, and was reassured to see they were waving gently, nudged by a westerly breeze. Good. Already the scent of Jud Linden, no doubt a little bit riper than it had been yesterday at this time, was being wafted along the ground toward the tent and the one nose out of four that could detect it.

Too bad, he thought, that he himself didn't have the kind of smelling apparatus that could provide him with volumes of useful information. He'd have to get his eyes and ears into the act by wriggling inch by inch up what remained of the slope. The ground was rocky, painful to knees, elbows, and ribs, but there was a profusion of sword fern whose fronds provided good cover and were easy to see through. About two minutes of cautious squirming brought his eyes to the level at which the tent, its platform, and its occupants came into view, providing he cocked his head at an uncomfortable angle in order to see between two gracefully curving fern fronds.

The scene that met his eyes was not one to gladden the heart of the wilderness marauder who had spent most of that day making life miserable for the actors in the scene. The two big men were seated on a low plank bench at the side of the tent, both wore grim expressions, neither appeared to be under the influence of anything but murderous thoughts, and each was busy cleaning a rifle. At the very moment of that first glance Bull paused in his work and raised his head. Jud's throat tightened and his heart did a disquieting flip-flop. Those black-browed eyes were glaring straight into his own.

But they *couldn't* be. The distance wasn't far short of

forty yards and Jud hadn't moved a muscle, not even to blink. He was right. In a moment Bull turned his head slowly to the right, then back and to the left, eyes probing the edge of the clearing. Jud couldn't have moved if there'd been a reward for it. A minute that easily seemed ten went by before Bull bent again to the task of plunging a metal rod up and down inside the barrel of his rifle. Muscle by muscle Jud relaxed. It was impossible to stay that tightly wound without having a stroke or something. With his muscles unclenched, his brain came back to life and part of it started asking rapid questions of another part which came up with no answers.

For one: could it be that he was watching a performance? Something about the way they were going at the gun-cleaning chore seemed to indicate they'd been at it for some time. And glowering around at the edge of the clearing—surely they couldn't intend to keep that up all evening. Was it all an act to put the fear of God into anyone who might be skulking in the forest, plotting new aggressions?

Why would they do that when they'd know by this time that their mysterious adversary was just a teenage kid? That would have been the first thing Yvonne would have told them. Or *would* it? She'd have had plenty of time to realize that her man would be anything but pleased to know she'd been gossiping over the back fence with a stranger who had "accidentally" stumbled onto his well-concealed pot plantation—even if the stranger were just a kid. No, she'd clam up, wouldn't she? Not wanting to get her butt kicked.

It made sense. So as far as the men knew, their unseen enemy could be someone just as big and tough and nasty—and well-armed—as they were. This was no act; they were alert, apprehensive, and dangerous. Jud wished his brain had stayed frozen a while longer. Why did it have to be so good at figuring things out?

Then why (no use trying to stop it now) didn't Bull have Bo out on the prowl instead of lying there dead to the world, a black-and-tawny mound on one side of the platform? Maybe they'd had him out for a reconnaissance already while Jud was dawdling along on his wide detour to get here. That was the happiest thought he'd had yet and he clung to it. If Bo had been on patrol already—maybe they wouldn't send him again.

His embrace of that hopeful thought was interrupted by the first voice to be heard from—Yvonne's—and in a moment she appeared, with a dramatic flourish, through the opening beneath the rolled-up tent flap, and for the first time in quite a while Jud felt like smiling. But not for long because he quickly realized that her exit from the tent was an entrance on the scene, which might cause complications. He couldn't hear what she said but he could tell it had been the equivalent of a flourish of trumpets—and nobody was looking at her but him!

She had got herself up in an outfit that was, to say the least, eye-catching. Gone were the grubby jeans and sweater, in their place electric-blue pants with flared bottoms, high-heeled shoes with something on them that glittered, and a low-cut watermelon-colored blouse with lots of frills. She'd piled her long reddish hair up in a pyramid that looked a little shaky. The finishing touches were dangling earrings, a gaudy necklace, and a collection of bracelets that probably tinkled or clicked or clinked or clattered with her movements.

Though Jud was no expert on fashion, he knew at once that Snory, who always looked just right, would never have rigged herself up like this. But it was obvious, even at this distance, that Yvonne felt really good about herself—happy, expectant. Hey, everybody, look at me! She said something, looking at Bull, who made a grunting sound and lifted the rifle skyward to peer through the open breech. Jud had a wild impulse to yell, "Turn around, you ugly meathead, and *look!*" What an explosion that would have set off!

The next moment poor Yvonne and her plight ceased to exist. Bo had suddenly raised his head, then rolled to the sphinx position and stared—so it seemed—straight at Jud, who knew by the way he moved his muzzle in small circles that his nostrils were twitching, testing the air. Was it that good old overripe, grungy Jud smell? And would he remember it? Ridiculously, he willed himself to give off ever more potent, ever friendlier emanations. Frustrating—like striving to *think* a sound, a call, a whistle. Such a thing could never happen, of course, but what followed was the same as if it had.

Bo scented the air a few moments longer, then got to his feet, revealing that, miraculously, he was not chained. At the same moment, Yvonne spoke again, louder, and Bull turned to look, then to stare. It couldn't have been better timed. Bo shook himself, glanced up at Bull as if seeking permission, and left the platform, heading into the middle of the pot patch. The plants were tall enough, bushy enough so that the dog disappeared from view. Jud searched frantically for a glimpse of him, a movement among the plants. He could be going in any direction, he told himself, with no thought of Jud on his mind. But he couldn't believe it. Any second now and he'd be looking up into those expressive eyes and . . . Good Lord! If that were to happen the jig would be up. Jud might be hidden, but Bo would be in plain sight from the tent, his tail would be wagging, and all hell would break loose.

A split second later Jud was slithering backward among the ferns, then, once he was out of sight, flipping sideways and rolling ten feet or so down the rocky slope before rising to his knees, eyes fixed on the spot where he'd just been. Mercifully it was a short wait. Like a dark genii, the dog appeared just to the right of the point Jud was watching, hesitated briefly, looked down, then launched himself. The next instant Jud's arms were around the powerful neck and he was laughing softly, and just as softly uttering idiotic remarks. "Hey, you good ol' century dog you! I smell bad enough to smell good, huh? You don't gotta be no guard dog, boy, jus' stick with ol' Jud." For reasons he'd never figure out it was much more satisfying to use backwoods English when speaking to a dog. He'd done the same with Bigfoot.

Speaking no kind of English at all, on the other hand, Bo made it amply clear that he too was happy with this unexpected reunion. But he did it with dignity. No messy puppy-style face licking for this aristocrat, no fawning, no ingratiating wriggles, no whining emotionalism. Just a dignified but heart-felt tail-wagging, an occasional nudge with his head to indicate he could still use a little more of this attention, and finally, a vastly benevolent, pink-and-white grin.

Jud could have gone on communicating this way indefinitely, but a sense of urgency nagged him. The dumbest thing he could do was stay here. Bull could have seen Bo in that brief moment when he'd stood there starting to wag a greeting. He could be coming, stealthily, this minute to investigate—with his rifle in hand. Jud got up, glancing apprehensively up the slope. Time to clear out, to go and retrieve his pack, and then . . .

Suddenly, for the first time all this long and eventful day uncertainty took hold. What *was* the next move? Where *would* he go from here? So far his luck had been good—incredibly good. A dozen things that could have gone wrong hadn't, and now he'd got ahead of himself, wasn't prepared to be where in fact he was. He hadn't really expected—just hoped—to get together with Bo so early and so effortlessly. But now, here he was, with Bo's head pressing against his hip—and there still was daylight left, close to two hours of it. So what was he waiting for? With winning cards, the last thing to do was fold!

Excitement seized him, buoyed him up like a balloon, and he talked stern sense to himself: You're pooped already, dummy. Want to step in a hole and break your stupid leg? But good sense didn't stand a chance. He'd be doubly careful, watch every step—but if this great dog was willing to follow him, put every possible mile between him and the fate he didn't even know was threatening him, Jud would walk until he dropped.

He took his hand away from Bo's head, took a step away —an illogical impulse to free the dog to make his own decision. "Bo," he said in a near whisper, "wanta come with me? Wanta go *home?*"

Those ears, forever at attention, twitched momentarily, infallibly catching the note of excitement in this human voice, and he rolled his eyes upward as if seeking in the face up there what he had heard in the voice: affection. Affection was something he'd known little of in his young life, but once he had encountered it in the voice, the body language, and the touch of this new human person, he knew it was something he wanted more of. Still peering upward, he grinned. He shook himself with particular violence. He wagged his tail. Bojangles was *ready*.

Jud's grin stretched across his face. "Okay!" he exulted, forgetting to keep the sound turned down. "Let's *go*." This couldn't have happened. It was too good to be true—like striking gold the first time you stuck a shovel in the ground. There had to be a catch.

There was. Fifteen minutes later he had retrieved the

pack, scarcely knowing how he'd managed to find it, with all that triumph and excitement boiling around inside his head. First thing he did was to get out his last chunk of pemmican, and share it with Bo. His impulse was to set off instantly. They could share the can of hash later, after they'd camped. But he forced himself to use his head, not to go off half-cocked. Out came the compass and map. He could hear the echo of Dad's voice: "Goin' in circles can make you dizzy and dead." Like Bo, Jud was well trained. The first half-mile would be easy because it involved retracing the northward curve of the route he'd followed earlier. After that there'd be a mile or so of strange ground before—with luck—he'd meet the trail he'd followed the day before. While he studied the map, Bo ambled down to the creek and returned with wet forepaws and a dripping muzzle.

They were ready now. Jud swung the pack up and settled it on his shoulders. That action might have been a signal, because the instant he did it the incredible luck went straight down the drain.

From above and behind a whistle sounded and he went rigid, heart hammering. It was the strong, penetrating sort of whistle a man expels between two fingers. It endured for perhaps three seconds, but in the first second he saw Bo's head snap around, ears pointing, followed by the rest of him. Again his head moved and he threw Jud a glance that looked like an appeal, but even as he did so his hindquarters tensed, gathered under him, and before Jud had time to force out a hoarse whisper, "No—Bo—stay," the dog was on his way, a black streak through the trees and up the steep slope beyond.

Bo was gone, and Jud was numbed by the dismal conviction that he'd not be coming back. The silence of the wilderness pressed down on him. That domineering, infuriating whistle had, for the moment, browbeaten even the birds into silence. His legs went suddenly tired and weak, and he sat down, pack and all, leaning against a rock and staring hopelessly at nothing.

Though he told himself it wasn't the same thing at all, he couldn't keep from thinking of old Bigfoot's death and the aching emptiness that followed. True, Bo wasn't dead, but he might as well be if Bull's awful plan for him worked out.

A minute or two of despair turned out to be his full allotment. Anger put a stop to it. Anger at himself, at Bull Durham. No, Bo wasn't dead, and neither by God was Jud Linden! So why was he sitting there like a wilting flower? Dammit, he wasn't finished yet. He'd lost a round, not the fight. There wasn't much left of today, but there was tomorrow! He lurched to his feet, which felt stronger now, and shrugged the pack into position. Things to do yet. Plans to make.

CHAPTER
8

Tomorrow came, as far as Jud was concerned, at five-twenty-two a.m. Dawn was little more than a promise. Here among the towering trees it was still dark as midnight, but where bits of sky were visible a pale light dimmed the brilliance of the stars.

He hurried out of his sleeping bag and into his clothes, impelled not so much by the frigid air as by a sense of urgency that made tolerable the thought of inaction. This was the day—the last day—the *only* day—the day he'd either beat the odds just one more time or face a future he could hardly bear to think about. There wouldn't be another chance.

Urgency or not, he followed all the rules of the trail, performed the housekeeping chores, from washing and brushing teeth at the icy stream to making sure all traces of himself received a decent burial. Breakfast was dried fruit and granola washed down with cold water into which he'd mixed the last of his chocolate-and-dried-milk mix. Not tasty but he was too impatient to unpack his tiny stove and wait while the mixture heated. Besides, this was no time to take a chance, however remote, that the smell of the stove and the liquid heating on it might be detected by a human nose. It was the same reason he'd eaten a cold meal the night before. That meal at least had been livened up by the sardines, whose can now rested in a plastic bag in his pack.

This morning he didn't hesitate for anything. No dawdling around in the hope that Bo might pay him another visit. The reason: he hadn't paid a second visit the night before, not after that peremptory whistle had called him away. Jud had kept hoping until well after dark. There could be only one conclusion: he didn't come because he couldn't. Either he was being closely watched or he was tied, and the reason for that was very likely Jud himself. It was certainly possible for Bull to have concluded that Bo's protracted absence the evening before was somehow connected with the phantom fiend of the forest, that the dog therefore should be kept under restraint. And to Jud it stood to reason that if Bo was tied last night he was probably still tied. No better reason for the phantom to be in such a tearing hurry now. He had to start with the first light in order to make his move while Bull and friends were still asleep. Once they were up and about he wouldn't stand a chance. Even at that, his own movements as he tried to free the dog could easily wake them and . . . But there was no point in even thinking about that.

By the time he was ready a pale light showed above the treetops and the birds were up and about, more or less musically discussing the day's agenda. Down here on the forest floor it was still more night than day, barely light enough to move with caution. Following the creek bed in its upstream direction, Jud soon passed from the shelter of the hemlocks and the day brightened. He could see the compass now, so he consulted it, though he'd studied his map minutely last evening and memorized the course he proposed to take.

He hadn't far to go—about half a mile. The stream bed made a semicircular detour here in its generally southwest-to-northwest course. At the upper end of the semicircle he would leave the stream and climb the spur of a higher-rising ridge, a height of scarcely a hundred feet, and there he should see the marijuana patch from a point just to the north of it. No way to tell by the map what the terrain there was like, but from what he'd seen earlier he knew a lot of vine maple and maybe elderberry grew fairly close to the tent site.

He hoped to find a spot that offered a view of the back and one side of the tent. Finding it was the easy part; getting to it would be tricky. Not just tricky—dangerous. Bo would be likely to sound the alarm if he heard a noise that didn't belong there. Jud's scent would be no help because it would be drifting northeastward, away from the camp.

The closer he got to his risky destination the more slowly he moved, watching where he put each foot, avoiding over-hanging branches. Luckily at this time of year there was no dry brush underfoot. But was it even possible to make *any* sound that would go unheard? He doubted it, but kept on going. He had no choice.

The last hundred yards of that half-mile took longer to cover than all the rest, and by the time his endlessly moving eye caught its first glimpse of olive-green canvas through lighter green leaves of vine maple, he was strung as tight as new fence wire and sweat was beginning to prickle underneath his shirt, though the air was still chilly. He con-gratulated himself on having left his anorak back there with the pack. With wild animal wariness, he sank down on the damp earth and inched forward. Twenty feet to go and he'd be at the very edge of the clearing where saplings had been cut and undergrowth cleared away to allow fifteen or twenty feet of open space at the rear of the tent, with a small additional clearing to accommodate the privy.

Eyes fixed on the goal—a slight hummock commanding a view of the tent's right-hand rear corner and enough of the platform in front to see whatever action there might be—he was making yet another reptilian advance on knees and elbows when in an instant he froze. A groan had blasted the silence of the morning. A human groan. But what did it mean? One of the men groaning in his sleep? In another second came the answer, and with it bitter despair. However many times he'd told himself the time would come when his luck ran out, he hadn't really believed it. But now it had done exactly that.

What he heard now was Yvonne's husky voice. "But sweetie—you *tole* me to wake you up! Kuh-*mon* now!" Another groan, and some mumbled words. Questions raced through Jud's mind. What was up? Why did Bull want to wake up right after dawn? But what did it matter? Gone was the chance to sneak closer, to turn Bo loose, and to get away. After all he'd done, all his careful planning—to have it all go to smash in an instant was a cruelty like none he'd ever known. Nothing to do now but squirm backward as silently as he'd squirmed forward. Get out of here—go somewhere—get *lost*, for all he cared.

Here came Yvonne's voice again, mournfully: "Oh, I *wisht* you din' have to go back so quick!"

Bull—savagely: "You think I *wanta* hike that bleep trail all the bleep way to Selma or further, and all the bleep way back for the bleeping *fun* of it?"

Thumping sounds indicated Bull was on his feet now, probably getting into his clothes.

"Well, sugar, you *sure* Jacko couldn't go instid of you?" The reply was another bleep and "Jacko—Jackass. He'd be lost inside of five minutes!"

"Well awright, I'll go fix you some breakfus', soon's I get decent."

More shuffling and thumping inside the tent, then Bull rasped, "Gawd, if I could get my hands once on the triple-bleep that's givin' me the hard time!"

So now Jud knew a thing or two he hadn't known before —not that it would do him any good. He knew that Bull was heading out at once for the nearest town. He knew that Jacko was staying here—he and his rifle, and his powerful arms, not to mention his eyes and ears. And he knew for sure now that Yvonne had indeed been afraid to tell her man about talking to a stranger. He waited a few more moments then inched forward again toward the hummock that had been his goal. Despair seemed to be giving way now to a sort of fatalism. Why not play the game out to the end—the end being when he'd have to run for his life. On he crept, all but plowing a furrow with his chin when he arrived an endless minute later atop the little rise in the ground.

Now he had just enough more breadth of vision to see that the shapeless mass on the deck in front of the tent was a sleeping bag with Jacko bunched up inside it. More important, just beyond that mass lay Bo. His head rested on his forepaws and from his neck a chain trailed off toward a front corner of the deck where it was undoubtedly secured to a staple or a spike. A groan might have relieved Jud's despair, but the price of a groan would be capture, or worse. He couldn't curse. All he could do was to storm inwardly, like many a loser before him, at the fickleness of Lady Luck who had dealt him what looked like a winning hand and at the last second snatched it away.

Now Yvonne appeared on the deck in front of the tent and busied herself with the camp stove that stood on the crude table there. Bo raised his head—hopefully, it seemed. The mass that was Jacko didn't stir.

More clomping and muttering from inside the tent and in a minute or two Bull emerged, gripping the straps of a pack in one hand. This he dropped as soon as he came out and without a word thumped to the edge of the deck and off it, heading for the privy which formed, with Jud's vantage point and the tent, a roughly equilateral triangle. Jud pressed most of his face to the ground, managing to keep one eye on the big man, just in case. As Bull disappeared around the corner of the little structure, Jud's attention shifted back to the deck in time to see Bo rise to his feet, stretch, and shake himself from stem to stern. His eye was on Yvonne and in a moment Jud knew why. The aroma of frying bacon had reached him now.

A minute or so passed, then here came Bull again, absentmindedly zipping up. Yvonne called out, " 'Bout ready, sugar. Want I should wake up Jacko?"

Bull snorted. "Set 'im on fire you might wake 'im up. Otherwise fergit it." He sat down at the table, waiting to be served. He cocked an eye toward his friend. "Jacko's the dude that slep' through near a whole hitch in the Army." He chortled appreciatively. "In the stockade, mostly."

He accepted the tin plate and fork she handed him, and once his mouth was full he pursued the subject. "You rilly wanta wake up ol' Jacko, just a whisper'll do the job, providin' what you say is, 'Drinks are on me.' "

Came then a muffled growl from inside the sleeping bag. "Go t'hell!" Bull roared with laughter.

Yvonne, quick to take advantage of his change of mood, said, "Well, he's awake now, so how's about lettin' me walk along a piece with you. Seems like I hardly even *seen* you." Shoveling food into his mouth, he shook his head. "You got no more sense than Jacko. Lose yerself before I even get out of shoutin' distance." "No I wouldn'! Find the way perfectly well from up there by that tree that got lightnin'-struck. Please, sweetie, lemme walk along."

Sweetie went on chewing while hope stirred a bit inside Jud's head. But it didn't stir much. Even if she did walk along there was still the formidable Jacko, who was awake now and close enough to the dog to touch him.

Yvonne's eyes were on her man, imploringly. No accounting for tastes, Jud thought. Then came the answer. "Oh hell, why not? The split tree and no further."

A few minutes later the two of them were angling across the clearing toward its eastern edge, Bull striding purposefully, Yvonne quick-stepping to keep up and chattering as happily as a teenage girl in a shopping mall.

No sooner had the forest swallowed them than a new movement seized Jud's attention. Bo. He had sat down again but now, while Jud's eyes had been on the departing pair, he had got to his feet again, turned part way around, and was facing directly toward where Jud lay hidden. And his tail was wagging furiously!

There was only one explanation: a freakish shift of the breeze had taken Jud's scent directly toward him. What next? Would he whine or bark? If there was a hand signal for "keep quiet" Jud had no idea what it was. A noise from the dog was all it would take to bring old Jacko out of his rumpled cocoon. One look at Bo practically *saying* that a friend of his was hidden out there would send the man diving for his rifle. And then . . .

And then, as if some weird telepathy were at work, the disheveled sleeping bag writhed and twisted, out came the smooth bald head and one massive, hairy arm, then the other. More upheaval and there stood Jacko on his bandy legs in all his hairy glory, clad in the bottom half of a set of long johns that apparently served him as pajamas. By pure blind chance his back was to the dog. He yawned with a noise like a crocodile's roar and used both hands to scratch here and there. Then he stumped to the edge of the deck and prepared to relieve himself over the edge of it.

In mind-shredding silence Jud watched, imploring preachments about manners, decency, and hygiene. In the end the message got through—either Jud's or one from Jacko's mother in his long-vanished childhood—and with a grunt the barrel-shaped man stepped off the platform and headed for the privy.

It took Jud no telling how many valuable seconds to answer such crucial questions as: Could this really be happening? Did he have the guts to try it? And if he tried it could he possibly get away with it?

And while he was asking the questions every muscle in his body was tensing, as if they knew the answers before his brain did. A few seconds more, while he watched with avid eyes—then the burly man stomped around the rear corner of the privy and disappeared from his view. Jud surged out of hiding, heart pounding as if he'd already run a mile.

The distance between his hiding place and the deck in front of the tent couldn't have been more than seventy feet, but it seemed minutes, and multiples of minutes, before a final wild leap took him to the middle of the deck where he dropped to his knees in front of Bo, who was wagging his entire rear end now. Forgetting his dignity for once, he gave his friend's face a welcoming lick with a wide, wet tongue.

Jud whispered that they were about to take off like a pair of scalded cats, fumbling at the chain meanwhile with fingers that felt like fat sausages. Bo, in his enthusiasm, was a long way short of helpful. He reared and lunged like a lamb at play, alternately tightening and loosening the chain, which was clipped to a loop in the training collar he wore, a chain itself that choked or loosened in turn, depending on the movements of the dog. The fastener was a simple spring-loaded hook, easy as breathing to operate providing both parties to the operation were relatively motionless.

It seemed to Jud enough time had passed to grow old and go to heaven before the clasp slid open and Bo was free and dancing around him. In an instant Jud leaped to his feet and cleared the edge of the deck.

The bound might have been a signal. As Jud's feet hit the ground running, a startled "Hey!" from the direction of the privy ripped the silence apart, followed by a shouted imprecation. Jud spared time for just one quick glance toward the sound. Jacko, his face contorted with whatever he was yelling next, was lumbering not toward the fugitives but toward the tent. After his rifle. The thought struck Jud almost in a dead heat with another: he's barefoot! A barefoot man stood a snowball's chance in August of catching a swift boy in lightweight hiking boots, and by the time he managed to put his own boots on the boy would be long gone.

He plunged into the trees at what he hoped would be a deceptive angle—toward the northeast—and with what breath he could spare told Bo, who was keeping up with no particular effort, "On our way, boy—goin' home!"

After a quick glance over his shoulder told him the tent

was no longer in sight he veered sharply to the left, and soon was backtracking along the course he'd followed after leaving camp. Only then did he slow to a walk. Bo slowed too and stayed by his left side, though no one had told him to. After a minute Jud stopped, listening. No sound of footsteps—and it wasn't likely there would be. Even if Jacko had got his boots on this quickly it was a hundred to one against his trying to follow. Not if he was as helpless in the woods as Bull had said he was.

About to forge on, Jud froze as the crack of a rifle went echoing from ridge to ridge. Crazy! Why would a man shoot at a target he couldn't see? Came then a second shot, and a third. Jacko wasn't shooting at him, he was signaling. Calling Bull back. Now Jud felt a chill of fear and without thinking put a hand on Bo's head. Comforting him? Comforting himself, more likely. The chill passed when he asked himself what Bull could do—or anyone else for that matter. The Kal was so vast it would be hard to find a herd of elephants in it, let alone a boy with a dog. All the same he set off again, picking up the pace a little. He'd pushed his luck too far already.

Soon they arrived back at his campsite, where he wasted no time in retrieving his pack and securing it in place after putting his compass in a shirt pocket for easy reference. To Bo he said, "Let's head for home. Okay?"

Bo made no answer, but his whole attitude said clearly that whatever Jud wanted to do would be all right with him. Jud thought about that as he strode along. It was a solemn kind of thing—that another living being would choose to follow him, not knowing, not caring, about what fate might have in store.

CHAPTER

9

The sun had sunk long since below Chetco and its companion peaks, and dusk was fading into night when Jud, with Bo pacing at his side, toiled to the crest of Granite Ridge and paused a few moments, looking down at the nearly level trail that linked the Kalmiopsis to the county road. It seemed at the very least a week since he'd climbed it in the other direction—and climbed it alone.

Shifting his pack a little to ease the ache of too many miles of rough terrain, he gave Bo's shoulder a pat. "Won't be long now, boy," he said, his voice sounding strange because he hadn't heard it for so long, and because the silence was otherwise so profound. Then he started down the slope.

In about forty minutes he turned off the road a hundred yards or so short of the graveled lane leading off it to the big, old white house among the trees. Here he could cut across the unused field to the house, but first he dropped to one knee and curled an arm around the big dog's neck.

"We made it, Bo," he said into the nearest ear. "We're home!"

The wave of affection that flooded him seemed a little hyper, a little overdone, even to him. But he couldn't help it. All day long, hour after hour, mile after rugged mile, the dog had kept pace, by his side where the terrain permitted but never far away except to go to a stream for water, never dashing off after animals of the forest, though he was bound to know they were all around. At rest stops he had sat when Jud sat, and at lunchtime gravely shared with him the can of corned beef hash, eating from Jud's only plate while Jud ate from the can with his fork. It was share and share alike—altogether right.

He would have been hard put to organize the words for how he felt. It wasn't as if he'd gone into the wilderness and found a dog—or rescued him, or *stolen* him—although he guessed he'd done all three. No, it was more that he'd gone there and been *chosen*—chosen above those whose life the dog had been sharing, those who had a legal right to call him their property. And having been chosen, he'd done a lot more than just get a dog. It was—well—like making an agreement—a contract. And a contract meant he had responsibilities. It was up to him from now on, whatever happened, to make sure this dog had a home and food, and a doctor's care when he needed it. Discipline too, and—there was no other word for it—love. And Bo, what was his part of the bargain? Well, that would be up to Bo, but Jud had a feeling he'd be thinking of a thing or two from time to time. Like sticking with his chosen friend on a long, tough trail when he didn't even know where he was going, or why. Doing it for no reason in God's world but that he wanted to be with this fellow creature he'd chased up a tree in the line of duty.

Jud felt a little silly, kneeling there like that. Solemn thinking wasn't his ordinary line of business. Probably it was because he was really tired. Another mile would have been one too many. Getting to his feet, he felt like an old man. Starting to stiffen up. Small wonder—he must have just about gone his limit this day, even though the last few miles had been a breeze, mostly level trail and then the stretch of road.

At his side Bo got up too, having sat down when the opportunity offered, and this time it seemed as if he did it a shade more slowly than usual. Could it be that he was just as tired as old Chosen Friend was? Smiling a little, he said, "Couple of minutes, boy, and we've got it made."

The field was humped in the middle, and not until they'd made it to the hump could he see the house plainly, and the low hedge that followed the long curve of the lane all the way back to the structure that was both machine and tool shed with a lean-to woodshed at the far end. Beyond that the lane made a sharper curve around the big vegetable garden. That curve was the parking place for the tractor-trailer. Ordinarily he'd be hoping to see it there; this time he was relieved when he didn't. So Dad wasn't home yet. Probably not until tomorrow. Good thing. Jud didn't feel up to facing him now. Making his peace with Carla was going to be tough enough.

In the big shed he switched on the light and dumped his pack, which was starting to weigh as heavily as the old man of the sea. Grunting with relief, he stretched cramped muscles. Bo's nostril's were twitching as he tried out the unfamiliar odors in this place. He cast an inquiring eye Jud's way and tentatively wagged his tail, signaling he was glad enough to be here, but what was going to happen next?

Jud grinned down at him. "Home," he said. "This is

where you live." He unrolled his sleeping bag and patted it invitationally. "Be my guest. Have a snooze. Be back before you know it, okay?"

With that he went out, making sure the door was latched. Then he squared his shoulders and headed for the house. The back door—to the kitchen by way of the utility room —was the one he ordinarily used, but this time he went down the lane toward what was called the front door even though it had originally been the side door, opening onto the living room. The door actually at the front of the house opened off the dining room to a porch overhung with honeysuckle. From the porch a walk led all the way down to the road and was almost never used. Visitors always parked near the side door and came in that way. That door too opened onto a long porch, this one festooned with wisteria. The top halves of both doors held glass panes into which were etched figures of noble stags in sylvan settings, in the style popular at the turn of the century. The only difference between the two porches structurally was that he and Dad had replaced the old wooden decking and steps with concrete.

Lights burned in all the downstairs rooms. Passing beneath the living-room window above the lane he could hear music from the television, and as he mounted the steps the sound covered whatever noise he might be making. The problem now, since Carla would have the doors locked, was how to get her attention without scaring her first. He peered in the window. She was sitting in the big bay window across the room which offered a view of both the lane and the road below. Her sewing basket stood beside her, but she wasn't sewing. Nor was she watching the television. She was looking out the window, through which almost nothing was visible at this hour.

Because she was a small woman who always wore dresses or sweaters and skirts instead of jeans like most girls and women he knew, and because recently she had taken to sitting in a dining chair because its straight back was more comfortable at this stage of her pregnancy, she struck him now as looking like a little girl who has been told to sit quietly and not make a fuss.

Not so little-girlish, and a shock besides when he caught sight of it, was what stood propped against the wall behind her chair. Dad's old shotgun. Jud doubted that Carla had ever in her life shot such a weapon or would even know how. But there it was, providing a few crumbs of comfort to a fearful woman.

He recalled his abrupt leave-taking—angry, resentful over something Carla had nothing to do with—without saying where he was going or for how long, and suddenly he was conscious of a faint glimmering of what it must be like to be Carla. Carla who sat fearfully in an empty house, maybe with scary things going on inside her, helplessly waiting for the men in her life to do whatever they were going to do.

This sort of empathy did less than nothing for Jud's self-esteem, and his conscience, which never missed a chance to turn up the heat, told him that whatever Dad chose to do to him would be no more than he deserved.

And in a moment long-standing resentments rescued him from guilt. After all, she didn't *have* to be such a mousy thing. She could at least watch the dumb TV—do *something* instead of just sit there like she was being persecuted. He tried to imagine Snory acting that way. Not a chance. She'd be stomping around with fire in her eye, itching for somebody to show up so she could land on him. Anyway he was tired and hungry and it was a pain to find the doors to his own house locked so he couldn't walk in when he felt like it. He ought to bang on the door—give her something to be scared of.

Next step was to sneer at himself, knowing he couldn't —and wouldn't come even close to doing such a thing, after which he went noiselessly down the steps and back up the lane, where he reversed course and began whistling loudly and more or less merrily until he climbed the steps again and called out, "Anybody home? It's me!"

There was an appreciable pause, then the sound of music ceased and he heard her footsteps, then her voice—uncertain, tentative. "Jud?"

"In person!" Jovial Jud, the Real Fun Guy.

She fumbled with the lock, opened the door, and looked up at him. Then, to his consternation, she whirled away, clapping her hands to her face, and went quickly back to her chair, obviously struggling to get herself under control.

Weeks later, when he was incautious enough to mention this bad moment to Snory, she went up like a rocket.

"Why, you *clod!* You big, brainless, unfeeling *clod*— what did you expect her to do—jump up and sing *Happy Days Are Here Again?* You've left her alone for two nights running and now it looks like a third one and she's scared to death you've fallen off a cliff or been chewed up by a bear, and she's scared anyway because she's about to have a baby and has never lived in a lonely house on the edge of a howling wilderness before, and Dad doesn't get home when he says he will, and besides all that she's climbing the wall with worry if you've ended up as a bear's breakfast it's *her* fault for not having stopped you somehow or called the sheriff when you didn't show up—or *something*. And *then* all of a sudden you pop up out of nowhere, bright as a little brass button, I'll bet—and *you* wonder what ails the woman when she has a tough time to keep from going to *pieces!* Well, I tell you if I was a bear I wouldn't take a single bite of you because I might get sick to my *stomach!*"

Leave it to Snory to let you have it with the bark on. However, an inkling of all this did get through to him at the time. Whether or not it was dumb of Carla to get so worked up when *he* knew all the time he'd be all right, he couldn't deny he'd put her through a tough time. Her suffering was real, regardless of what he thought about it. To his surprise he felt an impulse to do something unheard of, like pat her on the back, even to put a comforting arm around her. But he knew he couldn't begin to do such things. Instead he took a few steps toward her and stopped and said limply, "I'm—I'm sorry I stayed away so long."

His voice revolted him. Feeble—whiny—wimpish. But he couldn't stop himself. "I really meant to come back last night but—but something came up—and I just had to stay longer. I . . ."

Carla brought this disgraceful exhibition to a close by shaking her head violently. She thought it was disgusting too, he told himself, and how could he blame her?

The next moment he found out he was wrong. "No!" The word burst from her in a strained voice that didn't sound like her own. She snatched a Kleenex from somewhere and blew her nose with determination. "No, Jud! You don't need to tell me anything. You mustn't feel you owe me explanations. You *mustn't.*" He saw her back straighten, saw her take a deep breath. Then she faced him and smiled. Not a really natural smile, but a smile all the same, and he could tell a tremendous effort had gone into putting it there. "Tell you what," she went on brightly, "I'll just go see what's in the fridge. Bet you're starving. And I *know* you don't smell like the flowers of the forest.

Why don't you get out of those clothes and have a shower? By then I'll have something ready."

He mumbled something about not putting her to all that trouble, to which she replied, "My trouble is not having enough to *do*. Go on now, do as I say." With that she hurried to the kitchen, moving, he thought, even more awkwardly than when he'd last seen her.

Looking after her, he had to admire her a little. She'd got them both off the hook, and with no help from him. Then, while she made kitchen noises, he ducked down into the basement and got Bigfoot's plastic bowl and drinking dish which he'd stashed away just in case. There was also a metal container still half full of dry dogfood. Hurrying out to the shed via the side route, he found Bo lying on the bedroll, tail thumping. Putting food and water before his guest, who seemed to feel right at home, Jud said, "This'll have to do for now. Get you some good stuff in the morning." Then he sped upstairs to his room, stripped, and got into the shower.

At the kitchen table he sat down to a feast of cold chicken, fried potatoes, apple pie, and milk. Eight hours after a lunch of cold hash from a can, this was a memorable repast. He wanted to tell her so but feared it would turn out wimpier than the last things he'd said, so he put off trying by making sure his mouth never got empty.

Again she helped him out, this time by sitting down with a cup of hot chocolate and doing the talking herself.

"Elinor called," she said. Carla had never presumed to call her Snory, that being Jud's pet name. He'd known that all along but chose to call it another instance of her stuffiness. One more thing to feel guilty about now. But he couldn't sit there chewing in silence all night, so he swallowed and loosened a flood of words. "She okay?"

"Says she's fine. Crazy about the job. She's around the

stage people all the time—went to dinner the other night with the actor who's playing Mercutio."

Jud's knowledge of Shakespearean drama was shaky, to say the least, so he cagily ducked the issue. "She better watch herself with these actor types. Very unstable."

Carla chuckled at that. "She sent her love to you."

"I'll bet. Dare you to tell me what she really said."

Now Carla laughed outright. "If you put it that way, I will. She said if you weren't in jail to tell you hi."

He grinned. "That's more like it." He hesitated, took the plunge. "Heard from Dad?"

Her face brightened. "He called early today. Be home about noon tomorrow."

"He—uh—he ask for me?"

She nodded. "He did, but—" She peered into her cup. "I said you were outside somewhere."

Jud took a bite of pie to gain a little time, finally managed, "You didn't have to do that. But—but thanks."

"My good deed for the day. More milk?" He shook his head to the question, grabbed the opening. "I've been doing a good deed myself—anyway that's how I look at it—and it's why I've got to tell him myself—where I was and all that. But right now—" He put down his fork, took a breath. "Right now I've got to tell *you*."

She held up a hand. "No! Not if you don't want to."

"Well, I'd rather not, because you're not going to like it —but you've got to know."

She put her cup down very slowly, watching him intently. "All right," she said. "Tell me."

Nothing for it but to take the cold plunge. "I brought a dog with me—a *great* dog. I—rescued him from some men who were—well, never mind that—and he followed me home. I put him out in the shed."

She got up clumsily, as she did everything these days, and

took her cup and his plate to the sink, then turned around, leaning against the counter. "Please, Jud—I'd like to hear the *whole* story. May I?"

To his surprise he found that he wanted very much to tell her the whole story, wanted to make her understand how he'd felt impelled—*driven*—to take dangerous risks, to refuse to give up and come home even though he knew it was his duty to do so. And except for insignificant details he told everything—even the inglorious fact that for a time he'd been lost. He had to tell that because it was vital to the story. If he hadn't been he might never have known Bo existed—and that, in the light of all that had happened since, would have been a terrible thing.

What he didn't know as he warmed to his story, getting ever deeper into it, was that he'd forgotten such trivial things as how he felt about his stepmother, or she about him, and that he had become eloquent. She knew it, though. Her face, always expressive of whatever was going on inside, changed with every phase of the narrative—sympathy and amusement as he told about Yvonne, horror at the account of what lay in store for the dog, triumph and delight at the comeuppance of Bull and Jacko, apprehension at Jud's brushes with disaster. As an audience she left nothing to be desired, and the storyteller expanded accordingly. He concluded with an urgent plea that she make an all-out effort to conquer her fear and get to know Bo. "You'll love him," he wound up. "I guarantee it. He's that kind of a dog. And with him around you won't be afraid of being alone anymore." And finally the clincher. "And he'll guard the baby with his life—won't let *anything* happen to it."

She suppressed a shudder at the thought of her baby being anywhere near a big dog that was capable of being turned into a killer, but she failed to conceal the troubled look that had been taking gradual possession of her face. Her hands were clasped tightly on the table, and when she spoke her voice was troubled too. "However it all turns out, I want you to know one thing: I believe what you did—saving that dog from being turned into a—*monster*—was a great thing. It was *brave*—as brave as I used to hope I'd grow up to be and never did—and it wasn't just clever, it was—it was *brilliant.*

"But there's something else you've got to know, and try to understand. It's that people with phobias don't get over them by wanting to. Or trying to. They don't get over them by being told they're unreasonable and ridiculous and cowardly. They already *know* all that." She sighed dispiritedly. "Nonphobia people just can't understand somebody like me, and it drives them up the wall. They honestly believe it's just a weakness that we'd get over if we'd only show a little gumption."

She had been growing a little louder and more emphatic as she went along, something he wouldn't have believed possible, and now she was looking at him with a wry expression. "That's the way *you* feel about it. Please—don't bother denying it, because it's so. A phobia person can always tell. It's been happening to me all my life, so I know what I'm talking about. People aren't much good at hiding scorn."

There was nothing he could say to that, because it was all true.

"Well!" She straightened, looking determined. "I won't be giving you *that* speech again! It was only fair to tell you there's no cure for what ails me. I'm *positive* this dog is everything you say he is. And I'm *glad*, now that it's all over, that you took all those dreadful risks in order to save him. That's the absolute truth. But there's no use hoping I'll ever be anything but afraid of being near him. I'm sorry, Jud—truly sorry—but that's the way it is. Now—how about another piece of pie?"

A mere three days ago, Jud thought, he'd have shaken his head angrily and walked out, but now everything was different. She'd spoken right up, laid it on the line, and he had to think better of her. "No thanks," he said. "It was real good, but I had plenty." He couldn't give up. Not until he'd tried everything. "Couldn't you sort of *pretend* you aren't scared of him?"

She gave it some thought, or at least seemed to, but shook her head. "Who would I be fooling? Not you. Not myself, heaven knows. Certainly not the dog. He'd *know*."

Again Jud had to agree. Bo wasn't a dog you could fool. "Yeah," he said. "Guess you're right. But you won't have to cosy up to him or anything. I won't ever bring him in the house. He'll sleep in the shed, and I'll build a runway for him in *back* of it, to keep him in when I have to be gone. The rest of the time I'll be with him. Another thing . . ."

Laughing a little, Carla waved both hands to stop him. "Hold everything! No use you and me trying to settle all this. You know your dad will have the last word."

Now, in spite of himself, he did fire up. "You mean you'll get to him first! You'll tell him . . ."

"Jud Linden, you stop right *there!*"

He did stop, staring incredulously. It was like being lashed out at by a petunia. The surprise alone was enough to strike him dumb, let alone the totally convincing outrage in her voice. "Now just you listen," she went on. "I have yet to say *one word* against you to your father—and I *have no intention* of starting, now or ever!"

Jud didn't hang his head but he felt like it. There was just no way he could doubt she was telling the absolute truth. Not only that, though he might ignore it, he wasn't so dumb he didn't know she had covered for him in the past—more than once—and never said a word. "I'm sorry," he said, mumbling a little but getting the words out. "That was a rotten thing to say."

"Well, never mind. You're just all fired up about that dog, and I don't blame you."

Now she smiled. She was always at her prettiest when she smiled. She yawned and stretched. "Time for me and the little stranger to get to bed. Soon as I clean up here. . . ."

"No—you go on." He lunged to his feet, conscience-stricken. He knew she was tired at the end of the day, and here he'd been keeping her up to wait on him. "You go on," he repeated, "I'll be glad to do it."

She shook her head. "Thanks, but no thanks. You're the one ought to be worn to a frazzle. It'll just take me a minute."

"Well, if you're sure. Guess I'll go out first and see if—if he's okay."

At the kitchen door he turned. "Carla, I—" Right there he knew, to his horror, that he couldn't go any further. Forcing out one strangled word—"Thanks"—he fled into the welcome darkness.

CHAPTER
10

Next morning neither he nor Carla referred to what had gone on the night before, but it was by no means as if it had never happened. Jud wasn't at all sure what was different now, but something was. For one thing, she could make a few remarks without causing him instant annoyance, and while he was leery about exploring the thought very far, he kept having the uneasy feeling that there was more to Carla than he'd always thought—or anyway allowed himself to think. Maybe he was just getting used to her. High time.

It bothered him a little when he even consented almost cheerfully to go find some wildflowers so she could brighten up the house. Fortunately, he was able to absolve himself with the thought that the chore would fit right in with something he wanted to do anyway. This was to take Bo around the perimeter of the property, acquaint him with his area of responsibility. Jud had opened his eyes that morning with his mind made up. He wouldn't even entertain the thought that Dad's decision might go against him, once he'd heard the whole story. So Jud would go ahead as if the whole matter were settled, that Bo was here to stay.

Learning the boundaries of the place was an important part of being dog-in-charge, so off they went, Jud carrying a grocery box to put the flowers in. After the days of strenuous activity in the wilderness it was relaxing to stroll along on relatively level ground, nothing to do but keep an eye out for something blooming. Bo seemed to catch on to the idea from the outset, leaving his mark on strategic rocks and tree trunks, sniffing out the scents of other creatures and filing them away for future reference if needed. Next time he too could follow his own trail and grasp the concept of what ground was his and what was not. Compared with the many other things he had learned in his working life, it was puppy's play.

After the fastnesses of the Kalmiopsis, this was noisy country, though houses were few, some of them unoccupied this early in the season. Those were homes or cabins for city people who came for the fishing, camping, hiking, and boating. There were chainsaws to be heard, the occasional car on the county road and, farther off, the roar of the big rigs on the Redwood Highway, hauling freight between the towns and cities of Oregon and northern California. Unconsciously Jud kept an ear cocked for the low-gear whine and roar as the Peterbilt made the turn off the main road over at O'Brien. Few if any other of the big rigs would be making that turn. There was nothing for them on the winding country road.

That sound still had not been heard when he got back to the house. The morning passed. Carla fluttered around, putting the flowers he'd collected in bowls and vases which she placed here and there, then switched from there to here.

She dusted things that didn't need dusting, moved chairs an inch and a half this way or that. She peeked and poked at whatever she had in the oven or on the stove. And all the while she too was listening. Jud could tell by the way she'd stand motionless now and then, cocking her head like a robin on the prowl for worms.

Jud made good use of the time by clearing a space in a corner of the shed and building a four-by-four bed for Bo and filling it with straw robbed from the few bales that were kept for winter bedding for the asparagus and other plants. Then he turned his sleeping bag inside out and hung it over the clothes wire to air out. He didn't mind sharing it with Bo, but sooner or later rain would come and it would smell like wet dog forever.

Finished, he reached in and patted the straw enthusiastically. "Bed!" he exclaimed. "Bo—bed!"

Bo had been sitting up watching the proceedings with interest. Now he got up, peered at Jud's face. "Bed!" whooped Jud with feeling, leaning back on his heels, whereupon the dog stepped into the middle of this creation, tramped twice around, counterclockwise, and lay down. Then he looked up and grinned. Triumphant, Jud grinned too and stroked the broad head. It was something like a housewarming. Bojangles was now officially in residence. It then occurred to Jud he might have made the bed a little longer in case he had to come out here and share it. Might as well face up to it: he was as jittery as Carla was, and with a lot more reason. *She* didn't have anything to worry about, but before this day was over, *he* more than likely would have turned into the skunk in the cellar. Why didn't Dad *get* here and get it over with!

He didn't arrive until midafternoon. Jud had eaten lunch long since but couldn't remember what he'd had. At Carla's request he'd shifted a heavy bookcase an inch and a half to the left, then two inches to the right, where it looked *lovely*. In desperation he'd even gone out to the garden and hoed four rows of lettuce and four rows of beans, with Bo lending moral support, and was about to tackle the rhubarb chard when the whine-roar of the tractor-trailer set his nerves to twanging like a piano getting bashed. He dropped the hoe as if the devil wanted it, and ran for the shed, where he shut Bo in. Best to keep him out of sight until the right moment arrived, and it certainly wouldn't arrive until after Dad had made homecoming noises and greeted Carla. Especially the latter. Jud planned to give him plenty of time for that, in private. After that he'd be in a good mood and . . .

Jud halted himself there. It was unjust; Dad was seldom in anything but a good mood. Anyway, he'd be in a *better* mood. He thought of dashing to the house to alert Carla, but didn't bother. She was no doubt way ahead of him. Instead, he rushed back to the garden, and when the big rig, thundering in a low gear, wheeled around the shed and the garden to its parking place, there was the hard-working son of the house leaning on his hoe at the end of a row of chard, grinning like a clown.

With an explosive *shushhh* of the airbrakes, the rig came to a halt, and there was Dad, arm hooked over the window —grubby red baseball cap, blue western shirt, and a grin as big as Jud's. "Great gravy, boy—you gonna work your-self to death? Been at it ever' minute since I left. Right?"

"Well, I took time off for meals. Slept a little at night."

Opening the door, Dad swung down from the high cab. Tall, rangy, blue-eyed like Jud, wiry hair a couple of shades darker. Big muscular hands, big feet in the cowboy boots he favored when he drove. He paused long enough to stretch mightily before advancing a step or two to meet Jud who had moved too. As they shook hands Jud noticed he looked a little tired. "Bet you drove all the way through," he said.

Dad shrugged. "Took a little snooze up around Redmond." He looked toward the house and said a little sharply, "Carla okay?"

Jud knew he was wondering why she hadn't come running out to greet him. Couldn't very well tell him she was afraid of meeting up with Bo. "She's great. Think she's got something on the stove she can't leave."

Dad's eyes rested on him speculatively for an uncomfortable moment. There were times when he wished Dad wasn't so sharp.

"I'll go on up, see if she still knows who I am." He strode off toward the house. Jud stood, hoe in hand, feeling the heat from the big engine. He looked at the hoe with distaste. How could he go on whacking away at weeds? How could he do anything until he got through the ordeal that lay ahead? Until everything was out in the open? But he couldn't just stand there with his thumb in his mouth, and he had to give Dad and Carla a little time to say whatever married people said when they hadn't seen each other for a while, so he forced himself to go on hoeing.

He did three more rows and gave up. This was too much like waiting your turn at the dentist's. If he'd had any courage pills he'd have taken a handful. Lacking them, he marched up to the house with the courage of desperation and went into the kitchen. Dad was taking his ease at the breakfast table, legs thrust out into the middle of the room, a glass of beer at his fingertips. Seated opposite, Carla was laughing at something he'd said but stopped abruptly. Both turned to him inquiringly. "Sorry for butting in," he said, "but Dad, I've got to tell you something—uh—outside."

Dad's face took on a certain wariness. "I see." Then, "Something you can't say in front of Carla?"

"She's heard it already."

Dad threw her a quick look. "Plot thickens," he said.

She seemed to be examining her fingernails with interest and didn't look up, but she said, "You'd better go."

"Like that, is it?" He took a pull at his beer, set the glass down, and got up, heading for the door with Jud close behind.

"Victor!"

They both swung around. Her hands were on the table now, tightly clasped as they'd been the night before. "Victor—please—don't be hard on him. He's—he's a— he's a *fine* boy."

Dad's smile was affectionate and he said, "All right, honey, I won't kill him. But keep the door shut; don't want you to hear him beg for mercy."

Once outside, Dad said, "Where we going?"

Jud hadn't thought that far, but he said, "Out to the shed, I guess."

"First time I heard of a kid taking his old man to the woodshed."

Jud managed a nervous smile but got right on with the business at hand. "First I've got to tell you . . ."

"Hold on a minute!" No joke this time, Dad was dead serious. "Before we get into this whatever-it-is that's eating on you, and I get the idea you've got a list of confessions as long as your arm, I want to go on record with one thing."

"Oh—uh—sure." Not the brightest remark he ever came up with.

"I've got eyes," Dad said, "and there's nothing wrong with my ears. They told me in the last few minutes that something's happened. Things are different between you and Carla. Whatever brought it about I'm thankful for.

And if it's got anything to do with the evil deeds you're about to own up to . . . well, it's going to weigh pretty heavy in your favor. So all right, get on with it."

Jud took a moment to digest this and decided it would help some, but not much. "Glad there's something in my favor," he said, "because there's an awful lot that isn't. Anyway, I'll have to start at the end because . . . well, you'll see in a minute . . . and then sort of work backwards to the beginning."

"I usually like a story the other way 'round. But go ahead."

"Okay." Jud took a deep breath. "We're going to the shed because I've got a dog in there." From the tail of his eye he saw Dad's head turn quickly toward him, but he said nothing and Jud hurried on. "He's a great dog. You'll see in a minute."

At the shed door he called, "Hey, Bo—it's me!" Pushing in ahead, he put a reassuring hand on the dog's shoulder and added, "I brought a friend."

Bo was already adding sight of the friend to the scent and sound he'd picked up earlier. Man and dog regarded each other, Jud's eyes shifting anxiously between them. Dad ended the interlude with a low whistle to which the response was a quick twitch of those ever-alert ears and maybe the tiniest of tail movements. Then Dad spoke. "That is one—fine—dog."

A crumb of encouragement was enough for Jud. "He *is* —and he's trained for all kinds of things, and . . ."

Dad drowned him out. "And whoever's lost him is going out of their minds trying to find him."

"No they're not. There's no use trying, and they know it."

Dad shook his head a little. "You mind clearing that up for me?"

Jud was thinking fast. This wasn't the way he'd planned to get into his story—but then why not? "Well, if you lost a dog in the middle of the Kalmiopsis, how would you go about looking for him?"

"The Kalmiopsis! You've been up there?"

Jud nodded.

"*Alone?*" Until then he'd been pretty laid-back, but now his eyes were boring holes in Jud's head.

"Yes, but—but that's what I was going to tell you about."

Dad eyed him a moment longer, then strode across the cluttered shed to a workbench on the far side and dragged from under it a much-scarred sawhorse whose top was a six-inch plank. Pulling it closer, he threw a leg over it and sat astride. "Think I'll take this sitting down. All right, fire away."

Jud thought of finding something to sit on himself, but decided there might be some small advantage in speaking from a level above Dad's head. Anyway, he was too keyed up to sit still. "Well, it—" He had to stop and clear his throat. "It all started when I blew it again after—after I promised you. I—uh—jumped a guy. It was Roger Mattingly."

He told it all, sparing himself nothing even when he could have fuzzed a fact here and there to make himself look a little better. When he faltered to the end and stopped, he felt empty and dry. It was a little disorienting to look toward the smeared-up windows high on two walls and see a sky as blue as when he began. It seemed as if the earth should have made at least a quarter of a turn while he'd been spilling his guts. Bo, like a sensible dog, had put his head on his paws long since and closed his eyes, opening them only now and then when Jud's voice changed pitch with the excitement of some danger relived.

For his part, Dad had made no sound but an occasional muttered exclamation or the scraping of his boot heels on the rough floor as he shifted his position. Obviously he had ordered himself to refrain from any interruption, to hold his fire until the tale was told. Now it was told, and still he remained silent, staring at no telling what. High among the rafters of the vaulted ceiling a nest of hornets sent and received its endless stream of winged missiles through the ventilation louvers at the roofpeak. From a distant pasture came the call of a lamb and the ewe's reply. Here he was, Jud thought, in a place with the best of all men in the world, and the best of all dogs, and he felt as alone as he'd ever felt out there in the wilderness. Now that he didn't need to stand up anymore—and was too tired to anyway—he eased himself down to the nearest corner of the frame he'd made for Bo's bed, reached over, and rubbed behind the dog's ears. The response was a swishing of tail across straw.

At last Dad moved, swinging a leg over the sawhorse to sit sideways on it, knees together, leaning forward, hands under thighs to cushion them. Then he sighed, and that too was a lonesome sound.

"Time's come," he began, and then it was his turn to pause and clear his throat. "Time's come for me to give with the words of wisdom, and I haven't got any. If I was an educated man I might've read all the books on ethics and such and locked onto some answers. I doubt it, though. Lordamighty, Jud, they've probably never even written a book to cover all the pros and cons, why's and why-nots and on-the-other-hands in this cat's cradle you've been busy stringing together the last few days."

Obviously he didn't expect or want any comment. Jud kept his mouth shut and in a moment Dad went on. "If it could all be as simple as the TV thrillers make it out.

There's good guys and bad guys. The bad guys do the dirty to the good guys, and that's bad. That's terrible, because they're bad guys. But the good guys can do the dirty too— and the dirtier the better—to the bad guys. And that's good, because they're the good guys. And in the end there's blood a foot deep and the good guys win because they can do dirty stuff better than the bad guys. So that's it, and here comes the acid-stomach ad."

He snorted self-deprecatingly. "What all that was about is this: you stole a valuable animal from its rightful owner. Now wait a minute!" He flung up a hand to silence Jud's objection. "The second you unhooked the dog from his chain in the full expectation he'd follow you off, you committed theft. Theft is a crime. But you're one of the good guys. You did it with noble motives. But your victim is a bad guy, a lawbreaker himself. So what you do to him is okay. Get the idea?

"So now here *I* come. I'm a good guy. I obey the law, try to be a good example for my kids, earn the respect of the people who know me. Since I'm a good guy I feel it's my duty to march you up to the sheriff's office and say, 'Grab him, Mister Sheriff, he's a bad guy!' " He paused. "I do like hell! Because I know I'd have done the exact same thing if I'd been in your shoes!" Amazingly, he gave a little chuckle. "That is, if I was clever enough, and gutsy enough. All right, you know what that makes me, providing of course I don't follow my better nature and take you to the sheriff? That makes me an accessory after the fact, that is to say a criminal. A criminal is a bad guy."

He changed position again, stretching his long legs out and leaning back a little for balance, so that he had to sight along his nose to look at Jud as he added, "I trust all this is perfectly clear?"

"I—I *think* so," Jud said, ever hopeful. "I think you're

saying that since you can't sort out all that right-and-wrong business, and you'd have done the same thing yourself, then —then I might as well keep Bo."

"Nice try, but no cigar. We're still lost out here in the jungle. This dilemma's got more horns than a herd of antelope—and one of 'em involves Carla."

"But *she* said . . ." He broke off. Carla hadn't said he could keep Bo—but neither had she said he couldn't.

"Go on. She said what?"

"Well—she said you'd be the one to decide."

Dad sighed again. "Point is, I decided a long time ago. I knew about this fear of hers before I married her. I married her anyway—and that, to my mind, amounts to a promise. No dog. And I let you know about that. Now wait—wait —you had the floor for twenty minutes—my turn now. Point is: have you, or I, got the right to make her a prisoner in her own house, which is what she'd be with the dog on the loose. You can't . . ."

That did it. "But, *Dad*—I'm going to keep him out here. Build a runway in back of the shed—good strong one— and put a dog door in the wall there in the woodshed. And he'll stay in it except when I'm around to see he doesn't go near her. I can control him—I *know* I can. Already he does what I tell him. He *wants* to, I can tell! I can prove it. I can give you a demonstration that . . ."

Dad was making a pained face, fingers stuck in his ears, and he was saying, "I believe you—I *believe* you." Jud subsided, not so much because of Dad but because Bo was stirring uneasily under his hand. The loud voices were unsettling to him.

Now Dad seized the moment of silence. "Another thing. *I* don't know, and neither do you, just what all this dog has been taught. You know about the sentry part of it, but you don't know the command that activates it. You don't know what he's trained to do if somebody tries to get away instead of going up a tree like you did. You don't know who trained him and there's no way to find out. So you have no more idea than I have what other tricks he may be capable of."

Jud was showing signs of breaking in again and got a fast wave-off as Dad went on. "Dog like this is a loaded gun. I know—I know, he's everything you say he is— handsome and bright and friendly—but you can't be sure what's been programmed into his data bank. You punch the wrong key and somebody gets hurt. I don't want any- body hurt, and neither do I want anybody suing me for everything I've got. These are things you've got to take into account whether you like it or not."

To his dismay, Jud was caught without a ready answer. But there *had* to be one. His mind churned, and out of desperation came inspiration. What emerged wasn't really a falsehood but a sort of second cousin to one. "You didn't let me finish!" he explained. "What I'm going to do is take him to obedience class up in Cave Junction, and train him all over again. The guy running it is a professional dog trainer and he'll be able to find out about these things and tell me what to do about them. And he'll end up *safer* to have around than *not* to!"

Under oath he'd have admitted he didn't know if there was or would be such a class in Cave Junction, but there had to be one somewhere around and he'd find it. And he'd *go* to it. It would mean getting his driver's license in a hurry, but he intended to do that anyway.

Dad frowned, but nodded at the same time. "Seems log- ical—about the retraining. But it doesn't do anything about the other problem—theft of dog."

"But, Dad, what could I *do* about it? How could I take him back, even if I wanted to? After all the stuff I pulled on him, the guy would stomp me into the ground if I even got near him. And anyway I didn't *make* Bo come with me—he *wanted* to. It wasn't like stealing the guy's wallet or something. Wallets don't follow people home. Wallets don't let you know how they feel about you. And anyway—" With an effort he kept his voice from rising any higher. "Anyway, what those apes were going to do to Bo was worse than stealing him. Worse than *killing* him. Worse than . . ."

Dad flung both hands up, palms out, to stem the spate of words. "Hold it—hold it—you've made your point! *Several* points. I didn't say it was all black and white; nothing ever is. I'm just saying to back off a little, look at this thing from all sides. Maybe there are some answers we haven't thought of. Anyway—well, I'll think it over."

Quick switch: despair to hope. When Dad said he'd "think it over," it meant he'd really think. "Think *about* it" meant his mind was made up already.

The hope must have showed, because Dad said sharply, "Don't set off the fireworks yet. You're not off the hook— not by a long shot." With that he got up from the saw-horse, put one foot on it instead, and leaned his forearms on his knee. "Now," he said ominously, "we get down to the nitty-gritty—the only part of this whole Chinese puzzle that gives me no trouble at all. No argument about right and wrong.

"Okay. In the first place, I don't take at all kindly to your sashaying off into the Kal all by your bullheaded lonesome. Regardless of how it all turned out, you were dead wrong to go off there or anywhere else when you knew damn well I expected you to stay here and look after

Carla. But as I said earlier, I'm inclined to go easy on you because you managed to come to a new understanding with her after you got back. The other aspect of it—going up there when you knew it was not only dangerous but against all the regulations and all the laws of woodsmanship and plain horse sense—was just as bad. The fact that you saved Bo here shouldn't count in your favor because you shouldn't have been out there in the first place, and blasted well knew it.

"And there's another thing I bet never entered your head. What if I'd come home yesterday instead of today? Well, I'll *tell* you what. Within an hour from the minute I heard you were out there, the wilderness would have been swarming with men looking for you—rangers, deputy sheriffs, tracking dogs, helicopters—and *me*." He shook his head disgustedly. "And then you come waltzing out of there, lively as a cricket, with a stolen dog in tow. Well, nobody'd be more relieved than I would, and nobody'd be in more of a sweat to have your ears for my lunch."

He halted, mainly to catch his breath, Jud thought. "I—I get the picture," he said, mainly because he just about had to say *something*. At the same time he had a dreadful feeling that the worst was yet to come.

It was, but not quite yet. Now Dad took an aimless sort of turn around the shed, picking up a tool, putting it down again. Then he leaned his back against the workbench and went on. "You're going to get off easy on this one. All I ask is a rock-ribbed promise that you'll never, for *any* reason, go into the Kalmiopsis alone—that is, as long as you park your feet under my table. After that, it's your life."

Jud nodded, making himself look straight at Dad. "I promise, and—and I'll stick with it."

"You'd better. And now for the main event." The shed

echoed with the thud of Dad's boot heels as he walked back to look down at Jud, who felt like a moth pinned to a specimen board. "Your record on promises, I think you know, wouldn't even get you into a pool hall, let alone the pearly gates. You know what I'm talking about—you jumping whats-his-name—Mattingly. Not to mention the one, or two, or three before that."

He paused, and Jud thought maybe he was supposed to say something in his own defense. There wasn't anything, but he tried feebly. "I suppose it wouldn't help to say I'm sorry—really sorry?"

"Wouldn't help worth a damn. You've said it before—more times than either of us can remember. What you need is a lesson you're not going to forget for the rest of your natural life. And I've got just the thing in mind."

Dad's eyes were on him now, grim and implacable. Nothing to do but wait dumbly, like a steer in the slaughtering chute.

Dad went on. "You're going to punish yourself. That is, if you're man enough."

Jud was the rat hypnotized by the snake. He knew only one thing: whatever was about to hit him would be godawful.

It was worse than awful. "You are going to go," Dad began, every word receiving the same emphasis as the one before, "and face this Mattingly, and you're going to tell him you're sorry for what you did. *Wait*—I'm not finished! You're going to put your hand out and hope he takes it. . . ."

"Dad—my God, I—"

"And if he doesn't take it, if he spits in your eye instead, you're going to take *that*. You're going to keep your fists in your pockets, and walk away. With *dignity*."

"Dad! I can't *do* that. *No way*. You don't . . ."

"Can't—or won't?"

"*Can't.* Dad—I'd rather you'd take your belt to me—your fists—*anything.*"

"I know you would. Not going to oblige."

The very thought of doing this thing was unthinkable. It was crazy. It was impossible! He lunged to his feet, legs feeling weak and trembly. Bo stood too, sensing his agitation, looking uncertainly from one human to the other. "I can't *do* that—not in a million years. I'll do anything else—but not *that.*"

Dad cocked a hip, shoving both hands into his hip pockets, a typical stance. He looked as unyielding as ever, but—could it be there was a hint of softening? Some softening! All Dad did was nod his head a couple of times and say, "Yes you can. And you will."

Jud whirled, turning his back. He couldn't take any more of this. He'd leave home. He'd . . .

A big hand closed over his shoulder. He tried to shrug it off, but it refused to be shrugged. And there came that voice again. "Tell you something else. After you've done it—that is, if you haven't gone at it with that damned chip on your shoulder—you're going to get the surprise of your life."

There were plenty of cracks he could have made to that kind of a remark and he was trying to sort them out when a moist nose nudged its way between his balled fist and his side, insisting that the fist be opened so the hand could press against the furry head. And press it did. Hard, but not too hard for Bojangles.

Dad's hand unclasped and he said in his normal voice, "Guess that about winds it up—except for one loose end, and I'm not going to lay that one on you. Take care of it myself later on."

"What—what's that?" Jud asked, not really sure he wanted to know.

"The pot farm. Sheriff ought to know about it. No hurry, though. That Jacko got a look at you, so they know it's just a kid they're up against. Not likely they'd panic and bug out before harvest, which as I get it is late summer."

Tomorrow—late summer—never, Jud thought. What did one more lousy mess of pot matter compared with what he was up against?

CHAPTER

11

Jud spent the rest of the day learning, he thought, what it must be like to be a convict on Death Row. Execution up there ahead, but no date settled on. What Dad had sentenced him to do was unthinkable, but he spent all his time thinking about it. If you *had* to do a thing you *couldn't*, where did that leave you? Answer: climbing the walls.

Run away? Run away where—and do what? And with a German shepherd in tow? Ridiculous. And he certainly wouldn't run away without him. Get sick? Something infectious but not disabling? Leprosy? Oh shut up!

And anyway, what about the . . . the *other* thing? The thing he couldn't bear to think about. *Why* did everything have to be so hellishly *complicated?*

And so it went. Fortunately, dinnertime brought a whole new set of things to think about. Since dinner turned out to be roast beef with mashed potatoes and gravy, he realized his appetite hadn't withered entirely, and was contemplating a second helping when Dad looked over at Carla. "Okay," he said. "Tell him."

She looked startled, disconcerted, like a person called on without warning to make a speech. "*Me?*" she said.

"Who else? Go on—tell him."

"If you *must* have it this way! Jud, your father decided. . . ."

"Father, my eye! You laid down the law!"

"Victor, you know I don't *lay down laws!*"

"Well, is *somebody* going to tell me?" Time to step in here, Jud thought.

"All right—*we* decided," Carla said, "that you should keep Bo, and that I'll—handle my problem in my own way."

"That doesn't mean," Dad put in, "that you don't have to build the runway and all the other . . ."

"Victor! You made me tell it—so let me *do* it!"

"Oops!" said Dad.

"What I was *going* to say," she went on firmly, "was that I decided to try one—more—time. I—I don't think it will work, any more than it did the last time, but—but maybe then I didn't have the motivation I have now. So . . ." She had been looking down at her plate but now raised her eyes and gave each of them a look in turn. "So if you guys will just leave me to it—don't try to *help*—then maybe—just *maybe* I'll do better."

"That's my girl," Dad said. He waited a moment, watching her. "And that's all?"

"You told me to tell him, and I told him. What else is there?"

Dad tipped his chair back. He was enjoying himself. "Plenty," he said and looked at Jud. "What she didn't tell you was that for about half an hour this afternoon she—uh—*reasoned* with me. She said, among other things, that

I was being—er—stuffy. That was the word, wasn't it, dear?"

"Now *you're* telling it."

"She told me," Dad went on, "that I was trying to make you stick to a set of rules that not even *Jesus* would have laid on you. She said Jesus would have known right from wrong and have come down on the dog's side of it, him being the party whose affections were involved and whose future was at stake. Maybe his life. Have I got that right, honey?"

"If you say so," she replied, with a hint of asperity.

"I say so." Now he looked at Jud. "And I say something else: you're luckier than you know that your old man was smart enough to pick the right stepmother for you."

Jud stared into the mysterious folds of his napkin which was clutched in his fist as it lay on the table. "I—uh—wouldn't give you any argument on that. Carla, I—well, thanks."

So there it was—and the temptation was greater than a person should have to handle. Thanks to Carla, Dad was letting him off the hook—not about Mattingly but about the rest of it. But he was doing it for Carla, not for Jud, and dammit that wasn't good enough. Dad would never mention it, but if Jud grabbed this way out of the fact that—strictly speaking—he'd stolen a dog, the whole thing would hang there forever and stink, like a fish caught out of season.

Each word was as hard to put in place as a concrete block, but he achieved something like a sentence. He spoke to Carla. "Thanks a lot, I appreciate it—but I got to get square with the law."

"The *law?* Oh, Jud, you're not going to be stuffy too! You're not a . . ."

It wasn't polite to interrupt, but politeness didn't seem

very important just now. He went on looking at her, not Dad. It was easier that way. "I didn't think of it as stealing but—but I did steal Bo. No getting around it, so—I've got to report it."

"Oh—*no!*" Carla squeezed her eyes shut, then opened them to look from father to son with baffled annoyance. "If you're going to be just as hidebound as *he* is, I . . ."

"Family characteristic," said Dad. "I should have warned you." He gave Jud the merest ghost of a smile that managed—*how* could he do it?—to tell him that the underpinnings of the House of Linden were in good order. His tone, though, was one of deceptively mild inquiry. "What've you got in mind?"

"Depends," Jud said. He hadn't had anything in mind but now, suddenly, he did. "If I get my license pretty soon I'll go up to Grant's Pass and see somebody in the sheriff's office. Tell 'em I stole a dog. From a pot farmer. Then— then whatever they want to do about it is up to them."

Dad thought that over, nodded. "That should do the job. You can do it while we're gone."

Carla beat Jud to the starting gate by a split second. "While *who's* gone *where?*"

Dad pretended bewilderment. "Why—you and me— down to San Francisco!"

After a weighted pause she said, "Jud, if I murder him will you tell the jury why?"

Dad grinned happily and leaned back, hands cradling his head. "Before we know it we'll have a papoose to lug around—so why don't you and I kick up our heels a little? Take a week or so, go down to the big town. Let you buy a new outfit to wear when you're back to size eight again."

When the excitement died down, he explained. "This is Tuesday. On Friday I go to Crescent City and take on a

load for Vallejo. So you just come along. Lots of room.
All the other ladies say it's real comfortable. I can leave the
rig at the terminal. Then we'll do the town—shop a little
—eat a lot—ride the cable cars—see the sights—maybe
rent a car and go down to Monterey, Big Sur, wherever
you like.

"First thing tomorrow, Jud, you and I better go to the
DMV office so you can take the driving tests." He grinned.
"Give us a little leeway for another try if you flunk."

The pickup lived in the double carport at the rear of the
house next to the aging Honda that was Carla's before she
married. Jud went first to the shed the next morning when
Dad said he was about ready to go, and let Bo out for a
run. Then he went to the pickup, let the tailgate down,
and said, "Wanta *go?*" The dog crouched, looked eager,
but stayed on the ground.

"Come on, get in. Let's *go!*"

Same result. Jud was trying a different set of words as
Dad came out. "Looks like you don't know the password."

Jud tried other words and in the end leaped into the
pickup's bed himself and called, "Bo! Come!" Instantly an
effortless leap took Bo from ground to truck bed, where he
grinned happily. Obviously joyriding was high on his list
of entertainments.

"Little unhandy," Dad observed, "if you've got to do
that every time."

Jud jumped down, thinking hard. It had to be a signal,
not a command. Maybe his hypothetical dog trainer could
help.

Dad said, "You drive," and slid in on the right side.
"Okay, I'm the examiner. I had a fight with my wife this
morning and I'm in a stinkin' mood. So go by the book,

even if it seems pointless under certain conditions. Best way I can put it is this: drive like there's a patrol car on your tail, then you can't go wrong."

It was good advice, better than he actually needed, because the examiner was a relaxed sort who sized up Jud's abilities in the first five minutes and spent the rest of the time discussing baseball. When it was over, the officer said, "You're in luck, son. On odd-numbered Wednesdays in June I pass *everybody*. Anyway, the state sure needs your thirteen bucks. *Vaya con Dios.*"

Twenty minutes later Jud held, for the moment, the newest driver's license in Oregon. Dad's comment was, "Oh well, one more incompetent driver on the highways'll hardly be noticed."

Next he said, "By the way, I learned something about your friend back there." Meaning Bo. "He's put up a no-trespassing sign on this pickup."

"Oh Lord, what did he do?"

"I was keeping an eye on him through the back window. People went by—couple of dogs too. Not a peep. Then a fella started to rest his grocery bag on the rear corner there—while he got out his kegs or something. Meant no harm, but Bo didn't know that. He growled once. Real deep down. Kind of growl you wouldn't ignore unless you wanted a ride in an ambulance. Fella didn't dawdle."

Jud leaped to the defense. "Well, plenty of dogs guard their cars."

"Not complaining," Dad said mildly. "Matter of fact, it occurred to me that if I wanted to carry my life savings around with me I'd stuff it in a bag and toss it back there. Either he's been trained, or has the natural moxie to mind his own business until somebody sticks a hand in his cookie jar."

"*Said* he was smart, didn't I?"

"Several times. All the same, you'd better watch him like a hawk until you've seen him in about every situation there is."

Wednesday passed, then Thursday, and Dad made no further reference to the conversation in which judgment had been passed and punishment ordered. Jud didn't make the mistake of hoping Dad had forgotten, but wishful thinking kept suggesting that he might have such a good time on the trip that he'd come home bubbling over with the spirit of forgiveness, and . . .

Sure. And Jud might win the big lottery jackpot and live happily ever after. Friday morning came. Carla had loaded Jud with last-minute instructions on how to warm up the casseroles and other dishes she'd prepared for him, showed him where she'd posted a list of numbers to call in case of this emergency or that, and another list of things to do, such as water the house plants, and other admonitions essential to her peace of mind. Dad had brought the truck to the side of the house and loaded the bags in the capacious cab, handed Jud forty dollars for gas and groceries, plus a signed check for use in case of something unexpected. Last of all he lifted Carla, protesting, to where she could step in through the door of the cab. Climbing behind the wheel, he closed the doors and stuck his head out the window to look down on Jud. Only then did he mention what Jud had on his mind.

"Word of advice," he said. "Putting it off only means a longer time to dread it. When I get back I want to hear you bit the bullet." With that the mighty engine roared to life, and after that there was nothing to do but put on as pleasant a face as could be managed while stiffening the upper lip, and wave goodbye.

For a few desperate moments while the semi made its way down the lane, turned left on the county road, and in short order disappeared around a tree-lined bend, he entertained the wild idea of taking Dad's advice—now—this minute—get it over with. Anything was better than having a thing like this hanging over him like a poisonous cloud. But how to go about it? Go to Mattingly's house, knock on the door? Maybe his mother would answer, or his sister; what clever thing was he going to say to *them?* Probably Mattingly wouldn't be there anyway; he seemed to remember something about Mattingly getting a job at the Arco station down on the highway. No way you could do a thing like this at the place where a guy was working!

Better, maybe, to wait till after dinnertime and catch him at the Burger Bin, where he usually hung out with a bunch of other guys. But then what? Go slam-bang up to him and say, "Hey, man I just dropped by to . . ." Oh, forget it. He strode out to the shed and got furiously to work on the runway for Bo, who let him know it was a big treat to have company.

It was the beginning of a busy week. Jud worked all of the first morning on the runway—making measurements, digging postholes. Returning to his labors after a quick lunch, he came to a startled halt about fifty feet short of the shed door which he had left open, thinking Bo might as well run free when he had the chance.

The noise came from inside. It was a scrambling sound and a fairly loud *thunk* followed immediately by a softer *thunk-thunk.* More scrambling, then a *thunk* followed by no *thunk-thunk.* After that a pause followed by a *thunk* as loud as the first one. Now Jud was wearing a delighted grin because in between *thunk*s came the sound of hard panting.

Tiptoeing to the doorway, he eased his head around and peered into the shadowy interior. In the few moments it took for his eyes to adjust, the panting went on, but there was no movement. He could make out the dog's form, black coat blending into the gloom. He was sitting, back toward the door, facing the workbench at the far side of the big room. A few more moments passed and then he stood up, reached toward the floor and came up with a large object gripped in his jaws. He turned sideways then and Jud nearly let go with a whoop when he saw what the object was. One of Dad's big gum boots. Gripped by one side of its top, the boot's toe dangled down near the floor, forcing Bo to hold his head at top height.

The next move was to sidle about two feet farther away from the bench where he braced himself, swung the boot backward, forward, backward again—and then with a powerful neck-twisting motion he flung the boot up toward the top of the bench. It missed, striking with one *thunk* the outer edge of the bench, flopping to the floor with the second. In a flash he was on it, dragging it a few inches farther away this time and starting the whole process over again. This time it was a hit, a basket, a goal, a touchdown, hole-in-one—whatever he might have called it had he been a wordy sort of dog. One loud *thunk* and the boot stayed on the bench.

Jud was tempted to break the silence with applause but was tempted even more to find out what the next move in the game would be. He didn't have long to wait. Bo sat down again facing the bench, panting heavily. Then—at the count of what?—he stood up, reared with an easy motion, and lunged with his head, brought the boot down, the toe this time in the vise of his jaws. In this game, obviously, there was no penalty for using the jaws.

Jud would have sworn he'd made no sound—maybe it had taken his scent that long to cross the room—but suddenly Bo dropped the boot—very small *thunk*—and turned, tail already wagging. Jud assured him his new game was a real barn-burner, wished aloud there was some way to put all that dogpower and know-how to work at fence building, and got on with the job himself.

At about four he knocked off in order to put in a call to Doc Geraghty, who had been Bigfoot's veterinarian. From him he got the number of a dog trainer who had just started new classes in one of the buildings at the fairgrounds in Grant's Pass. Jack Hamlin, the man's name was, and Jud got him on the second try.

Keeping it short, he explained what he wanted, and after a few moments' thought the trainer said, "Tell you what. Why don't you bring your dog up before class starts—ten after seven, say. I'll take a look at him, see what we can come up with."

He did more than that. Jud was there with Bo well ahead of the appointed time, a little nervous because he didn't know what to expect. The trainer arrived in a van with wire mesh compartments built into it to hold dogs, and put him at ease at once. A square, solid, competent-looking man of about forty, he said, "Call me Jake, everyone else does." His keys jangled. "Come on, I'll open up, turn on some lights."

Once inside the building, which was a livestock exhibition hall, and smelled like it, Jake said, "What's his name?" Jud told him and he bent down, ruffled the fur of Bo's neck, patted his shoulder with authority and spoke his name. "Bo—how ya doin'? Good-lookin' devil, aren't you?" To Jud he said, "Take the leash off." Then he stepped in front of Bo, facing him, and made a motion with his left hand, so near to imperceptible that Jud nearly missed it. Promptly, Bo sat, watching him intently. No question in his mind that this man was in charge. In quick succession then, Jake put the dog through a series of maneuvers, silently, using only hand signals, then brought him back to Jud. "No doubt about it—he's been to college. You say you found him?"

"That's right." He hoped Jake wouldn't demand more information. But the trainer merely nodded. "Well, you found yourself a gold mine on four legs. Lot of hours gone into his training." After a moment's thought he went on. "Only way to make a dog lose a skill he's been trained to perform is to see he doesn't use it. Just like you and me; we may learn Japanese or something, but if we never use it we lose it. I'd suggest you come to a few classes, just to teach yourself the basics. Then you can keep him on his toes just on the routine stuff. As for the sentry commands, it's highly unlikely you could give them by accident, so I wouldn't worry about that."

This suited Jud perfectly and he got out his wallet. Jake waved it away. "I can't take money when your dog's already trained. Tell you what—Bo here can pay for training *you*. I'll use him to show the class what they're aiming at. Make 'em work harder."

And so it was arranged. Jud attended that evening's class and came again the following Monday and Wednesday. It was on the Wednesday that he and Bo covered themselves with glory—of one sort or another.

It was difficult later to believe that so much could have happened in so brief a time—a matter of seconds for the first part of it. In the first two sessions Jake had been directing the people to work their dogs in a large circle, or in straight lines facing each other. This time, for reasons he left unexplained, he formed them in two circles, one inside the other and moving in opposite directions.

When it happened, Jud's line—the inner one—had its dogs seated facing inward, while the other circled around them. In that circle was a part-Doberman male in the hands of a young man in his early twenties. Both man and dog,

Jud had decided, were real pains. The dog seemed to be a troublemaker and the man was one of those who refused to accept criticism. Twice Jake had mildly admonished him to keep his dog under control and each time he had argued about it, claiming to have done just what he was told to do.

It was not without reason, then, that Jud felt a little uneasy when the command came to "Halt—sit your dogs!" and chance placed the troublemaker almost directly behind the seated Bo. Jake explained to the halted line what was going to happen next. Then he started with the command, "Outer circle, Walk your dogs!" The line started, and with that the other dog made a lightning slash at the rear end of the unsuspecting Bo.

The shepherd's reaction was an outraged roar, a lightning whirl, teeth bared, toward the flank of the Doberman, now dancing forward at the end of his leash in a swift avoidance of vengeance.

Jud, swiftly enough but not half as swift as either dog, tightened his grip on the leash, started to pull back against the momentum of Bo's lunge. Then, astoundingly, the leash slackened as Bo again whirled and sat down in the exact spot from which he had leaped. It took Jud a moment to comprehend it. Incredibly, Bo had remembered at the launching of his counterattack that he was under discipline. Bo was a dog who played by the rules.

At that instant came Jake's voice, full blast: "Halt your dogs!"—followed by, "You with the Doberman, step out of the line!" The man didn't obey. Instead he turned angrily. "Yank that *shepherd* out of the line! He started it all!"

Now it was Jud's turn to whirl. Now came the old familiar roaring in his head, the rush of adrenalin commanding him to fling himself at this lousy, lying pile of . . .

It was a near thing—so near that it left him weak and

shaking. What would have happened had he not held a leather leash in his hand? What if he hadn't shown barely enough sense to wonder what Bo would do if this chosen master of his had thrown himself into combat with someone who appeared to be a threat to him? And what if it hadn't occurred to him, at the last possible instant, that if his dog could get himself under control, what use would he have for a master who couldn't?

With an effort that hurt physically as well as mentally, he forced himself to stay where he was, gripping the leash as tightly as if it were a lifeline in a stormy sea. And he kept his mouth shut, except to drop to one knee and give Bo a tremendous hug and tell him he was a dog in a hundred million.

Meanwhile the instructor, pleasantly but with steel in his tone, was saying that an obedience class was no place for a dog who would attack another. He thrust some greenbacks at the young man, saying, "Here's your money back. This class will resume *after* you've taken your dog out."

The man took the money, then balked, looking mulish, and stood his ground until the other owners began raising their voices from mere murmurs to audible demands that he get out—take off. In the end he took his grudging departure and the class went on.

Going home, Jud put Bo on the seat beside him. No second-class compartment for the prince of dogs! Besides, he felt so great he just had to have somebody to talk to. He couldn't really talk to a dog about the exhilaration that was filling his chest with tiny bubbles like champagne, but he could pat him now and then and beam at him vibrations of triumph and jubilation. It was birthday and Christmas and the Fourth of July rolled into one, and the world was washed with a golden glow that no one could see but him.

He'd finally done what he'd never really believed he could do—at last kept the promise he'd made over and over again —at last kept his temper in check—at last kept his fists to himself—at last won the toughest fight there was—the one with Jud Linden.

It cooled him off a bit to reflect that he'd never have done it without Bo to set the example. But then again, he *might* have. And next time, if there *was* a next time, he'd do it or choke!

Thirty minutes later he rounded a curve and saw, just ahead on the left, the oasis of light that was the Burger Bin. There was time for only the briefest of thoughts, time for only the quickest of reactions. He signaled, braked, turned, and the gravel of the parking area was crunching under the pickup's tires. He pulled to a stop beside the last of the cars parked in a straggling row in front and to both sides of the nondescript structure that housed the little restaurant. He cut the engine, pocketed the keys, and the thought leaped at him from the shadows like a mugger: it's not too late—back up—back out—take off! Promptly he squashed the temptation. Probably never again would he be so convinced that the impossible was something he could handle. He stroked the neck of the prince of dogs and said, "Take care of stuff, boy. Back in a minute." Then he climbed out, shut the door firmly, and set off toward the circle of light cast from inside the Burger Bin, a circle inside which a gaggle of figures lounged, leaning against car doors and fenders. Familiar figures, most of them.

Maybe Mattingly was not among them. The thought shifted quickly from hope to frantic disbelief. Mattingly *had* to be there. This chance wasn't going to come again. After this something would always come up, some reason not to . . . And then he saw him. The screen door had opened, slamming back against the front wall, and there was Mattingly silhouetted against the light behind him. In one hand was a large Pepsi with a straw sticking out the top. Now or never—now or never. Jud's mind was stuck there, a cracked record. He took a deep breath and moved forward into the light. He was aware that a voice nearby halted in mid-sentence, and of a shifting of shoes in the gravel as the figures came erect, heads turned. Ignoring them all—this was no time for any dumb hiya-guys routine—he made straight for the front stoop with its three steps, none of them quite level. Mattingly advanced with his usual swagger and had taken the first step down when he saw who was coming, and froze.

Jud halted just short of the steps, looking up. Now the only voices to be heard came from inside. It was a stage—curtain going up—and he hadn't learned his lines. His plan, insofar as there was a plan, had been to get Mattingly off to one side and speak privately, but at this last possible moment an impulse seized him, and he knew it was right. After all, he'd jumped the guy in front of everybody, so it was only right to . . . "Been looking for you," he began, not loudly but clearly. No chance he'd not be heard. "Came to say I'm sorry. I didn't have any business leaning on you like that—I was way out of line—and if you hadn't tripped you'd've probably cleaned my clock for me. And I'd've had it coming. So. . . ." He thrust his hand out and up. "So would you shake hands and—and could we be friends?"

There! He'd done it—got the words all out without garbling anything badly. Nothing to do now but wait, and if Mattingly chose, as Dad had suggested, to spit in his eye, he'd grit his teeth down to the gums and *take* it. He could do it, and he *would* do it.

The wait seemed to go on for measurable minutes and was probably seconds. Then the older boy, staring down at him as if he couldn't believe any of this, slowly transferred his drink from right hand to left, hesitated yet another moment before saying, "Well hell—why not?" Out came his hand and grasped the one offered.

Somebody broke the silence behind Jud. "Well hey—good goin'."

Mattingly came the rest of the way down the steps. "Well, everybody knows I don't hold a grudge," he said expansively—news to almost everybody present. Then he gave Jud a clap on the shoulder. "You're okay, Linden. Takes guts to admit you're wrong. You were right about one thing: 'nother minute and it'd've been you on the deck, not me!"

Same Mattingly. Same mouth. But Jud didn't care. He was still up on his cloud. Mattingly could say whatever came into his head.

Right there the amazing thing happened. The habitual blustering air suddenly slipped and for a second Jud had the unsettling feeling he was looking at the inside of Mattingly, who said in a low tone the others couldn't hear, "That's a lie. You had me whipped. I know it an' you know it."

"Maybe. I'm not bragging about it." In a moment he added, on an impulse prompted by Mattingly's own performance, "Now *I'll* admit something. I didn't apologize because I wanted to. My dad made me do it. Only—once I got started I *did* want to do it, and . . ." He broke off, aware that silence had once more descended on the parking lot, and looked around to see half a dozen or more faces watching intently. He grinned at Mattingly. "What say we give 'em a chorus of the old school song? Little soft-shoe number too?"

The other waved a disparaging arm. "They ain't worthy of it."

Then they all started yacking, as if it had been forbidden

until now. "Well," Jud said lamely, "guess I better get on home. See y'around."

"Damn betcha!" said Mattingly.

Not until Jud was back in the seat, getting a warm but dignified welcome, did the recollection of Dad's words break over him like a wave in the surf. "If you don't go at it with that damn chip on your shoulder you'll get the surprise of your life." And that was exactly what had happened! He'd have bet everything he owned or would ever own against Mattingly's humbling himself and accepting a bid for friendship. Was Dad psychic or something? Or did he just know a lot more about people than a person might want to give his old man credit for? Whatever the answer to that, he could hardly wait to tell Dad that the bullet he'd bitten turned out to be a caramel bonbon.

CHAPTER

12

After that the days remaining slipped by as smoothly as a trout in a stream. Everything was easy, nothing was too much trouble. He finished the runway, cut a hole in the back wall of the woodshed and installed a dog door, and stretched heavy pigwire over the runway's top, just in case Bo should turn out to be the sort of canine Houdini he knew some dogs could be. He took Bo to Doc Geraghty for the usual inoculations, having no way of knowing whether he'd had them already. He also got Bo a leather collar with an identification tag on which he printed his name and address.

Other chores and odd jobs followed. The skies were clear ahead as far as he could see from his vantage point in this never-never land masquerading as the real world. On the day before Dad and Carla were due back it went spectacularly to pieces.

This was the day for doing a week's worth of house-cleaning in a couple of hours—no sense in making his bed and cleaning up the kitchen when there was nobody around to see it but himself. By midafternoon the place was respectable again and it was time to go out and buy groceries to replace a lot of things he'd been consuming at a great rate.

His intention was to go up to Cave Junction where there was a supermarket, and if he'd done so everything would have been different. It was one of those insignificant, spur-of-the-moment changes of direction made by millions every day and remembered only when something dreadful happens. At the main highway he turned right instead of left, deciding not to drive the eight miles to Cave Junction but to go to Grimes's, the mom-and-pop catering to local people and weekend fishermen and vacationers. Old man Grimes's prices were higher but Dad liked to patronize him now and then, just to help keep him in business.

Parking between two other pickups facing the storefront, which sported a veranda and Old West–style hitching rail, he instructed Bo as usual to "take care of stuff," and went in. He filled his basket in short order and headed for the front counter where old man Grimes presided over an antique cash register. As he was passing the three big refrigerators holding soft drinks and beer, a man slammed a door shut and swung around in his path, six-pack of beer in hand.

Only fast reflexes kept Jud from dropping the basket, and he felt as if a fist had knocked the wind out of him. He was face to face with the man called Bull who looked, up close, even bigger and tougher and more menacing than he had looked at a distance. Besides all that, he hadn't had a bath in quite a while.

The urge to whirl and run for his life was irresistible, and he had to *make* himself believe that, as many times as he'd seen this man, the man had never seen him. And even when he managed to believe it, he had to fight the craving to simply put his basket down and get out of there. But why chicken out when there was no point in it? Instead he detoured around Bull and went on to the counter, trying to look like a person without a worry in the world. Old man Grimes took his time as usual, muttering to himself as he rang up the purchases and made change coin by coin.

Jud, meanwhile, stood slightly sideways, hoping to keep track of Bull's movements. The old man was about to hand him his change when Bull loomed up behind, plucked his beer down on the counter, and rumbled, "Hey, Daddy-O, where-at's the bak'ry stuff?"

Jud could tell by the way Mr. Grimes refused to look up or give any sign that he'd heard, that he didn't take at all kindly to Daddy-O. Not until he was completely finished with Jud did he look up and quaver, "Now, sonny, what was it you wanted?"

Gratefully Jud swept up his purchases and made a swift departure. His main objective was to put as much daylight as possible between himself and the alarming Bull. Starting down the steps of the veranda he suddenly tried to stop, stumbled, and nearly fell with the force of his momentum. If blood could run cold, that's what his was doing. There at the side of *his* pickup, decked in jeans and a frilly see-through blouse, stood Yvonne. She was talking animatedly to Bo, but she was obeying the rules—no petting. Bo was looking down at her, tail majestically wagging. Jud could have parked beside any of half a dozen other vehicles— but no, he'd chosen to pull in beside Bull's high-slung pickup, which he'd have recognized if he'd had his head in the game. Worse than that even—why—*why* hadn't he given a thought to Yvonne once he'd set eyes on Bull? Now he didn't have a grasshopper's chance in a henhouse of getting out of this in one piece—and all because he was dumb—dumb—dumb!

But there was nothing to do but try, no way to go but forward. Fortunately, her back was toward him and she was absorbed in her one-way conversation. He made it to the driver's door, wrenched it open, flung his grocery bag on to the seat—never mind the eggs—and hurled himself in after them. Precious seconds passed while he fumbled in pockets for the keys, then fumbled some more to find the right one, and before he found it there she was, just inside the still-open door, big eyes looking up at him, hurt and accusing.

He couldn't bring himself to push her away so he could close the door and get moving, and he couldn't back up without knocking her down with the open door. He was helpless as a beetle on its back.

"Well if you ain't a sneaky one!" Yvonne was saying. "All them things you done, an' you surely to Jesus made my man godawful mad, only he don't know who he's mad at."

"He'll know just any second, Yuhvon, if you don't stand back and let me . . ."

But there was no stopping her. "An' you took an' stolen our Bo right out from . . ."

"I didn't steal him—he followed me. So please just move back and . . ."

"Cross your heart you din steal him?"

"Swear to die, Yuhvon! Now *please* just . . ."

But it was too late. Like the shadow of doom Bull came slouching through the doorway, halted at the top of the steps, peering down. Apparently he didn't make the right connections. Maybe hadn't yet identified Bo. Saw only that Yvonne was talking to somebody in a pickup. Maybe his mind was slow, but not so slow he wouldn't put it all together at any moment. Now he clumped on down the steps, moving closer, scowling as he strained to make out who it was in the pickup.

Jud's mind raced, arriving nowhere. He could run, and maybe Bo would follow. But maybe he wouldn't, and Jud couldn't leave him. Anyway, how could he leave the pickup either? No telling what Bull might do to it, seeking revenge. No, this was the end of the line, and all he could do was get out and on his feet—at least have room to move a little.

He slid out of the seat, moving Yvonne aside as gently as possible. His feet were on the ground, but now Bull was there, towering above the two of them. Even now, he hadn't made the connection.

Jud thrust the uncooperative keys into a pocket and sidestepped deftly to the open space between the two vehicles. Then it happened. He saw the big man's squinting eyes flick from himself to Bo—back to him—back to Bo again—before he let out the outraged bellow of a bull tormented beyond enduring. There were words in the bellow. Not pleasant words. He thrust his grocery bag into the arms of Yvonne, who staggered with the force of it, and with a jerk of a thumb sent her scurrying toward his own pickup. Now he concentrated all his long-festering fury on Jud. "YOU! *You* give me all that mis'ry? Stinkin' snot-nose-punk like you! Time you was taught a bygod lesson!" He took a step forward, reached out with a massive arm. Jud did a quick backward shuffle. "Better not," he said. "Too many people watching." None were, but it was a safe bet there soon would be, with the noise Bull was making.

"Hah! Ain't bit on that old dodge since I was in short pants." He lunged again, grabbed empty air.

Now two middle-aged men did step out on the veranda.

"It's no dodge," Jud said. "Two guys wondering what you're up to." Watching Bull's eyes, he saw indecision. He couldn't be dumb enough to beat up a teenage boy in a public place and think he could get away with it. But even if he tried Jud knew himself to be quick enough to stay out of reach. Goad him a little, keep him busy. Any minute the audience could get bigger. Patrol cars passed now and then, and Bull was in no position to attract the law's attention.

Hoping to remind him of that, Jud said suddenly, "How's the crop coming along?"

It took a moment, but Bull wasn't too dumb to know a threat when he heard it.

Looking murderous, he let go with another string of obscenities and ended with, "Know what's good for you you'll forget you ever seen any crop."

Now came a distraction in the form of Yvonne, back from putting the groceries away. Looking worried, she jiggled her man's arm. "Leave 'im be, sugar, he don't mean you no more harm. He says Bo just follud 'im off, an' I believe him." She jiggled him again. "Please, hon, they's folks a-watchin'."

Without even looking at her he said, "Go git in the truck." Now he took two strides toward the rear of Jud's pickup, growled, "Get lost, punk. I'm leavin'. *With* my dog."

Jud threw a quick look at Bo, who looked confused, worried, uncertain. Jud tried once more, desperately. "You forget about Bo, I'll forget about the crop. Lot of trouble to go talk to the sheriff."

This brought a sneer from Bull, who had now reached the side of the pickup, put a hand on it. Bo didn't react, except to look more nervous still. "Go on, punk—*talk* to the sheriff. Talk to the FBI if you wanta. Talk to the goddam *CIA*—but I'm tellin' ya this. First lawman comes snoopin', y'know who I'm gonna shoot first? *This dog!*" With that he lifted Bo from the pickup and started for his own.

Only then did Jud, frozen by the cold-blooded threat, shake it off and hurl himself into action. Moving swiftly, he planted himself in his enemy's path. All this got him was another cursing and the ignominy of having to back up. Though he was desperate enough to attack, there was no way to do it. If he swung a punch, or even a well-aimed kick, he was as likely to hit Bo as the man who held him. He flicked a glance toward the veranda. The two men were scrambling back through the door they had so recently come out of. Going for help, maybe? To call the Patrol? His eyes switched back to Bull at the instant the big man lashed out with a kick that could have crippled him had it connected. Jud's backward leap brought him slamming against the side of Bull's pickup, his head striking one unyielding surface, his right hip another, and in a moment the big man had stepped to the front of the vehicle, then around to the driver's side where he jerked open the door, thrust Bo into the seat. The door slammed, the engine leaped to life, and Jud managed to whirl away just as the vehicle zoomed backward, turned, and roared off in the direction of California.

The last thing he saw of its occupants was the face of Yvonne, her left hand held up near her right shoulder where Bull couldn't see it. Her fingers were waggling an apologetic goodbye.

Within a few seconds the truck disappeared down the highway, leaving Jud in the middle of the parking area, torn between murderous rage and utter desolation. Outthought, outmaneuvered, outbluffed by a big dumb slob who wasn't fit to call a great dog like Bo his own! He drove home at a suicidal speed but got there in one piece in spite of himself.

He spent the rest of the day and the early part of the night working himself to a state of exhaustion. With ax and wedge he went at the pile of uncut tree sections at the far end of the shed, turning them into stove wood at a whirlwind rate. It slowed down the endless process of thinking, remembering, regretting, hating, but didn't make it stop. In the end he sank one cutting edge of the double-bit ax into a log and walked away, avoiding even a glance at the runway and the rest of his handiwork.

At the house he stuffed cold beans and stale coffee cake into his mouth, paying no attention to what it tasted like. Then, with no pack, no map, no compass, he headed into the woods, following the west fork of the Illinois in the direction of its source across the California line. Kept going until darkness threatened to close down, and even then turned back only with illogical reluctance, reaching home about ten o'clock beneath a brilliant moon he barely noticed.

An hour in front of the TV set watching an old horse opera completed the job and he staggered to bed where he slept like the uneasy dead, dreaming cheerlessly. He woke at eight, later than his habit, ate a breakfast that made more sense than his meal of the night before, and tried to settle down and *use* his head instead of just hitting it with a hammer.

It seemed a sure thing that Bull had turned around and headed back up the highway, probably aiming for Selma, which had to be the jumping-off place for the return trek to marijuanaland. He and Yvonne might even have made it all the way back before real dark, so now poor Bo was probably right back where he'd been before Jud ever set eyes on him, half a lifetime ago. Only this time he'd bet anything, Bull would keep him tied up. No use even to think of going to the law. He didn't doubt for a moment that Bull would carry out his awful threat. Bo was as much a hostage now as any of those people seized by terrorists.

And there was no use either in thinking of going back up in the Kalmiopsis and repeating his recent feat. Nobody's luck could stand that kind of stretching. Probably just get himself shot along with Bo. So what to do—what *could* he do? Nothing—except to tell Dad the whole lousy story. Maybe he could come up with something.

Almost at the stroke of noon the Peterbilt made the difficult turn into the lane and roared up and around to its resting place. Dad was out of the cab and on the ground by the time Jud arrived from the house. With a wave and a "Hi, young'un!" he strode to the other side and lifted Carla down. It seemed to Jud she was even bigger than the last time he'd seen her. But could that be true in just a week or so?

She looked at him, smiling happily, glad to be home, then suddenly the smile vanished. "Something's wrong, isn't it?"

Dad took her arm. "If something's wrong we'll hear about it soon enough. Let's get you in the house and sit you down with your shoes off."

She didn't move, went on looking closely at Jud, then beyond him toward the shed, whose door stood open, back to Jud again. "Bo," she said. "Where is he?"

"He's gone."

"Gone? Oh no! Gone where?"

"It's—it's a long story."

"In the *house*," Dad said. "Sit down while I make some coffee—then hear about it."

"I'll go in," she said, "but *I'll* make the coffee. There's nothing *wrong* with me!"

In the kitchen, while Carla started the coffee maker and

Dad got out cups, Jud made bright conversation. "How was the trip?"

"Great," Dad said. "We did go down to Big Sur."

"Oh, the *scenery!*" That from Carla.

"She shot three rolls of film," Dad said, grinning. "About a dozen shots with the lens cover on."

A little more of this and that, and then they were both sitting with the coffee, looking at Jud, and Dad was saying, "Okay, boy, let it out."

"Well, first the good news." Trying for something other than a note of bleak misery. "I went and—did what you told me to. And you were right. It turned out great. Real good."

After a time, thinking this over, Dad said, "I owe you one, Jud. Wasn't *sure* you could do it. I should have been."

Jud couldn't help getting a lift from this, at least enough to get him started on the bad news. No matter that he'd relived the scene countless times in the last twenty-four hours, it was still hurtful to tell about it, but he worked his way doggedly through it, leaving out no detail of his own stupid, thick-headed, *feeble* performance.

When he had finished it was Carla who was first to leap into the silence. "Oh, Jud, how dreadful for you! How *heartbreaking*. But you mustn't—you *must not* blame yourself. What in heaven's name could you have done against a brute like that?"

"She's right," put in Dad. "One hundred percent. I know how you must feel—but no use beating up on yourself about it. Thing is to figure out what can be done."

Jud shook his head gloomily. "I've thought of a hundred things, none of 'em worth spit. Whatever we'd try to do would only get Bo shot. That devil would do it. I believe him!"

Dad thought a while, finally nodded reluctantly. "Suppose you're right. You'd be a better judge than I would. Damn! What a rotten piece of luck!"

"Do you think," Carla began, a troubled sympathy clouding her eyes, "that is, maybe not now but a little later, you could think about getting another dog—as much like him as possible?"

For a moment resentment flared at the idea any other dog could take the place of Bo, but it died as swiftly. Carla wanted to help. And was trying. And coming from her it meant a lot. He replied awkwardly, "Appreciate it, but—but I guess not."

Dad said, "Time might come when you'd change your mind. If so you can count on me to help you get what you want. Meanwhile I'll try to think of some answer you haven't thought of. Not likely, but you never know."

Jud tried to act hopeful, and worked hard at listening to an account of their trip, and the talk about how short the time was getting before there'd be a new little Linden in the house. None of it eased the dull ache of loss.

It didn't help to learn that instead of being around for a while Dad had to take off early the next morning on another job. The final proof that Jud was beyond all help came that evening when Snory phoned. "Just calling to find out how many of you are there at this point," she explained. Even talking to her failed to cheer him for long.

What did help a little was the idea that came some time in the night. He thought of Jake, the dog trainer. Not that Jake could tell him what to do about his impossible problem, but those lessons had an appeal for Jud that he couldn't altogether explain. What if he'd go back to the class, ask Jake if he needed an assistant? Without pay, of course. Somebody who'd be willing to do whatever dirty work there was, and in the process learn about handling dogs and training them. Maybe it could turn into a job. Maybe, if he had any talent for it, into a career. In time, he'd have known so many dogs that Bo would be only a memory.

Doubting it, he went to sleep, and later on he dreamed. He dreamed that somebody had died, and though he asked over and over again nobody would tell him who.

CHAPTER
13

Later—much later—he dreamed that a violent machine was jouncing and shaking him and harshly hooting in his ear. He clung to sleep but the machine was too powerful by far. He hurtled into wakefulness and there was Dad with a big hand on his shoulder, jouncing and shaking. "Get *with* it, Jud. Wake up—I need a little help."

He opened his eyes. Dad's face was up there, mouth moving, and beyond him, where the window was, there was light. Not much, but enough to show a new day had come. There was time to wonder, irrelevantly, how it was that out on the trail he could wake with first light and be on his feet in thirty seconds while here in his bed it took a revolution to get him up. With a superhuman effort he sat up, peered blearily upward. "Okay—okay—what's the deal?"

"Little problem with the rig. Needs two wrenches and

four hands. There's a big crescent wrench there in the shed. Grab it and come on out to the truck."

"Okay."

"Sure you're awake now?"

"Uh-huh."

"Lemme see your feet hit the deck."

Jud groaned, flung the covers back, and made a big show of bounding to his feet. "This is cruelty to a minor. You know that?"

"I'll hate myself later. Be out there in five minutes or I'll *show* you cruelty."

Not until Dad had left him to scramble into pants, shirt, and shoes did Jud's mind play back to him the sound of Dad's voice. There had been something odd about it. Unnatural. He wasn't bright enough right now to figure it out. He spent a full minute finding one tennis shoe, which had landed in his chair when he kicked it off and was covered by his shirt. The search woke him up enough to remember that Dad could get pretty impatient when something delayed the start on a job, so he stumbled down the stairs and hurried out to find Dad leaning in over the coupling between the tractor and trailer. Hearing Jud's approach, he turned quickly around, stared, and snapped, "Where's the wrench?"

"Oops! Forgot—still asleep." He loped back toward the shed. As he approached he heard a high, shrill sound that brought him instantly awake. It had to be real—he couldn't possibly be dreaming anymore.

He wrenched the door open and immediately staggered backward, nearly falling as eighty-odd pounds of fur-covered muscle and bone catapulted into him from the still murky interior of the shed. Bo's whine turned into little falsetto yelps—a ridiculous sound, but no more ridiculous than the noises that came from this chosen master of his who was laughing like a hyped-up hyena while he weakly fended off the onslaught. In the end he flung an arm around the muscular neck and clamped it there until sanity returned, and with it silence.

"D'you mind running through that again? I missed the opening." Dad was standing there wearing a grin like a horizon. "He gave *me* a reception, but it couldn't hold a candle to that one."

Jud returned the grin, with compound interest. "Nothing wrong with the rig, was there?"

"Good thing. I'd get no help outa you now."

"How—how do you suppose he found his way back?"

Dad shrugged. "How does a little bird get here from Guatemala? How does a salmon find the right river to swim up?"

Now another voice was heard. "*What* is going on?" Carla was in the open back door, clutching a terrycloth robe around her.

Dad raised his voice. "Return of the prodigal."

"Not *Bo?*"

Hearing his name, Bo rolled his eyes up toward Jud's, as if begging to be excused, and trotted toward her, but about halfway there he halted and stood slowly wagging his tail.

There was a noticeable silence, then in a muffled voice she said, "Ohhhh—Bo!" Jud couldn't see her eyes, but her voice suggested there might be tears in them.

Dad said wonderingly, "If I wasn't seeing it I wouldn't believe it. He *knows* he mustn't go any closer."

Nobody said anything else for a time, all pondering the phenomenon of Bojangles. Then Jud did an abrupt switch to something he could better understand. "Food!" he blurted. "He must be starving!"

This he soon rectified by means of a can of Alpo with an egg mixed into it.

It was difficult, a little later, to sit with the others and eat his own breakfast. Full of the wonder of it, he couldn't keep from speculating, often with his mouth full, about one thing after another.

How long had it taken Bo to make the trip? What time did he start, and from where? Had he leaped from the pickup somewhere along the way back to the camp? Did he take off when Bull had run the pickup into its hiding place? Had he escaped the first night? Yesterday? Last night? Had Bull felt confident enough to turn him loose, or did he somehow get loose by himself?

Thinking of that, Jud suddenly muttered an exclamation. How dumb could he get? Not until this moment had he thought about it, but Bo was no longer wearing his collar. It hadn't been real tight, so maybe he could have pulled out of it. This thought pulled him up short; if Bo had left the collar behind he'd also have left the tag with Jud's name and address. So now Bull would know his name and where to find him. Could mean more trouble ahead.

He decided to worry about that some other time. Right now he thought he'd go try himself out at putting Bo through his paces with hand signals. Dad left right after breakfast, but not until he'd had a last-minute "confabulation," as he called it, with Jud by the side of the semi. "Carla's not due for two-three weeks," he began, with no preamble, "but it could happen earlier. You can never be sure. I told her I'd phone every night to check up. But I'd feel easier if you'd stick pretty close to home. If you go somewhere in the evening—like the dog class—just check with her first. I made her promise to tell you if anything funny's going on—pains or whatever. And don't waste any time getting home when you *are* gone. That okay with you?"

"Sure." Jud grinned. "Bo and I, we'll look after her. Don't worry."

Dad opened the door of the cab, then turned back, smiling a little but dead serious too. "Tell you something. Whatever I worry about, it won't be my boy Judson. Not anymore."

He thrust out a hand and as they solemnly shook Jud was aware, to his surprise, that his hand no longer felt so very small, and that he didn't need to raise his eyes very much at all to look straight into Dad's. So what about it? Why did noticing things like that suddenly set off a fierce kind of ache way back somewhere between his throat and the roof of his mouth? What was the *matter* with him, for cripes sake?

But when Dad let go his hand and said, "So long, then. See you in a week," the best he could manage in reply was a nod. And while the rig roared and growled its way down to the road he stood watching it go and wondering if he'd go on thinking Dad was the greatest if he came home every night, like other people's fathers. He didn't get to answer himself because Bo thrust his nose into the hand that hung down within reach, and Jud had to pay attention.

That night after dinner Carla joined him in watching the last four innings of a ball game. He knew she didn't care a lot for baseball, so it seemed only fair that afterward he should sit and talk a while. Not about anything in particular, just this and that, but it was a comfortable time, and in the end, as might have been expected, Jud found himself talking about Bo. He relived bits of the miracle of finding the dog in the first place, then about the training classes. From there he rambled on into the future, what he might do about becoming a trainer. Moonshine, maybe, and he knew it, but she listened so well and with interest that just couldn't have been faked, that it was hard to make himself shut up.

He did, of course, probably because he was getting sleepy, and a silence fell, only mildly disturbed by the ticking of the little brass clock on the mantel. Finally Carla sighed—more of a contented sound than anything else—and said, "Isn't it strange? Bo's been around such a little while—but already everything's different. For all of us."

Jud thought about this and wished he could tell her that he knew just what she meant, and why. But there was just no way to talk about things that meant so much, no way that he knew anyhow, or could have managed to say if he did. In the end he chickened out, let a fake yawn turn into a real one, and got to his feet. "Guess it's time to hit the sack," he said. "I'll go put Bo in and be right back."

He'd reached the doorway to the kitchen when she stopped him with a word. "No!"

He turned back questioningly as she rose awkwardly from her straight-backed chair and stood facing him. "Jud, this is terrible," she said, "after all the work you did building the place for him. But I don't want you to pen him up anymore. Not on my account."

Dumbfounded, he stared at her. "Are you *sure?*"

She nodded, with solemn emphasis. "I've thought about it long and hard—and I'm sure. I decided that while I'll probably never be able to pet him and play with him and all that, I do know one thing absolutely: that dog would never, *never* hurt me. So—let him go free."

In his room Jud undressed in an absent-minded way. "*I* didn't convince her of that," he told himself. "*Dad* didn't do it. *Bo* did it." Maybe he'd build him another bed—this one on the front porch. Maybe someday she'd decide to let him come inside. There wasn't anything that dog couldn't accomplish!

In the morning, after asking Carla three times if she felt all right, he set off in the pickup for the sheriff's office in Grant's Pass. It was true that the situation was different now that Bo had run away on his own, with no urging from Jud, but even so he'd stolen him the first time and he meant to get everything clear on the record. And the sooner he did it the sooner he could feel at ease. Three times Carla assured him that nothing dramatic was about to happen.

"Well, at least I can leave Bo here," he offered.

"For heaven's sake, what for? *He* can't take me to the hospital!"

He laughed. "Well anyway, I won't dawdle around."

As it turned out he was home again by the time it would have taken just to get there. Luck had it that as he passed the Burger Bin he caught sight of a sheriff's patrol car parked among the other vehicles in front and made a quick decision. Why not? Wouldn't cost a nickel to try. At the first turnoff he reversed direction.

The sheriff's officer in his neat brown-and-tan uniform was easy to spot among the T-shirts and jeans. He was alone in a booth, long legs stretched out under the table. Red hair topping a rugged, homely face, blue-gray eyes that swept Jud quickly from top to bottom and back as he approached.

"Excuse me." Jud felt more awkward than he'd expected to. "I was heading for Grant's Pass to—uh—report something, and I saw your cart out front, so I . . ."

"So you decided to get me to save you all that trouble. Well, that's what we're for—to help out the taxpayer." He took a swallow from his coffee mug, peering up at Jud over the rim of it. Then he set it down with a thump. "You *are* a taxpayer, I suppose?"

"Well, not exactly. . . ." Jud didn't know what to make of this man, whose face offered no clue whatsoever.

"Never mind. You will be. If you live. No way out of it. What's on your mind?"

At this point there was an interruption in the guise of Doreen, who had been hustling the burgers and shakes here for as long as Jud could remember. She plunked a burger and fries down in front of the officer with her usual "watch-the-plate-it's-hot" and peered at Jud. "Hey Jud!" she greeted him. "When you gonna bring that good-lookin' old man of yours in here?" Doreen, who must have been well over forty, made a big thing of being man-crazy though she'd been married for years to the foreman of the sawmill at Cave Junction.

He grinned at her. "Bring him in soon's he gets back. Just took off this morning."

Now the officer spoke to her, tipping his head toward Jud. "Friend of yours, Doreen?"

"Known him since I had to wipe the ketchup off his chin."

"He a criminal type?"

"Wouldn't turn my back on him. Gonna have somethin', Jud?"

"Thanks, I ate already."

"Have a seat." The deputy lifted the top off his sandwich and smeared it with mustard. "I'll eat. You talk."

Jud talked, keeping the account as short as possible. It was like talking to himself, for all the impression he seemed to be making on the officer, who made the burger and fries disappear with astonishing speed, pushed the plate away, and called for Doreen, who whooped from across the room, "Raisin pie's all gone. Try the banana cream."

"You talked me into it." Without a pause he flipped a

small notebook and pencil from a shirt pocket and opened the notebook. "Okay. Full name."

"Judson D. Linden."

"Age. Address. Phone. Date of occurrence." He printed the answers swiftly in heavy black strokes and went on writing. Doreen brought the pie and filled his coffee mug. He ignored them both and continued to write. Obviously he'd been paying more than close attention. Finishing, he put the notebook aside, drew the pie toward him, and began on it while Jud watched, hypnotized. Wasn't the guy ever going to *say* anything?

He was. Finishing the pie and taking a slug of coffee, he leaned back and favored Jud with a level gaze that might have contained the barest hint of a smile. "Tell me now—if you were me would you believe the story you just told me?"

Jud squashed the impulse to leap to his own defense. Something was telling him he'd end up looking silly. "I guess," he said, doing his best to match the impassive gaze across the table, "I guess it wouldn't be easy."

Now the officer did smile. "Gave me no trouble at all. Us smart cops just can't be fooled. Where is this dog now?"

"Outside in my pickup—my dad's, that is. You want to see him?"

"Corpus delicti, isn't he? Always got to look at that." He stood up, put a dollar on the table, and picked up his check. At the cash register Doreen gave him his change and he dropped a nickel on the counter. "That's for you, sweetie," he said. "The service was incomparable."

"Oh, you *shouldn't*," she simpered. "See you next time."

In the parking area the officer stood silently for an appreciable time, regarding Bo, who had stood up, the better to wag a greeting to Jud. At last he said, "Well, son, I can see how this fella might lead you into a life of crime. He's a beauty."

Jud's reaction didn't differ much from a mother's whose child is admired, but it wouldn't do to let it show. Besides, he was getting a little worried about how all this was going to end.

An answer came immediately—or anyway what seemed like an answer. "If you'll just step over here to my car . . ." No question he expected to be obeyed.

Jud stepped as requested, apprehension growing. Was he going to be fingerprinted? Given a confession to sign? Handcuffed?

At the car the officer opened a door and from a side pocket extracted a map, proceeded to spread it out on the hood. "Reckon you can pinpoint the location of that marijuana grove for me?"

"Oh—uh—sure." No little relieved, Jud took the yellow highlighter pen offered him and bent over the map. There was the Kalmiopsis, on a slightly bigger scale than his own map, and he resolved to get one like this for himself if he could. It took only a few moments to zero in on the Bull Durham estate and circle it with the highlighter. For good measure he drew a line from there to the pickup's hiding place and on eastward in the direction of Selma.

Handing back the pen, he asked hesitantly, "You going to raid the place? You'll look out for the girl, won't you?"

The officer answered only after he'd finished carefully refolding the map. "That'll be up to the sheriff. My job's to question people, get the facts, write reports."

"Oh," Jud said, feeling vaguely let down and relieved at once.

"What you mean, 'Oh'?"

"Nothing. I just thought, you know, there'd be some exciting stuff too."

"Oh! You mean gunning down bad guys and all that! Sure, I do a lot of that too. Killed a couple last week. Crippled another. Wednesday, that was—no, Thursday."

Jud's grin felt a little sheepish. "Well, anyway, you going to write a report on me?"

"Absolutely." The deputy returned the map to its pocket and slid in behind the wheel. "Time I hit the road. Got a few baddies to shoot on the way in to the office." He slammed the door and laid an arm over the edge of the open window.

Jud's consternation at being left hanging in midair, so to speak, must have showed because the man's face broke into a grin that made him look younger than before. Probably he'd been intending to relent anyway.

"What'll happen," he said, "is you'll be notified of any action that's going to be taken. If it comes to a warrant for your arrest it'll be served by one of us."

"Oh. Uh—any idea how long it might be?"

"Not the foggiest." The deputy flipped a couple of switches on the dashboard and his radio receiver hissed and spluttered. Then he turned the ignition on and the engine idled quietly. Not until Jud stepped back, raising a tentative hand in farewell, did the man smile again, this time in kindly-old-uncle fashion. "Tell you what I'd do, Jud, in your shoes: I wouldn't sit by the phone, or run to the mailbox every day. I'd just get on with my life. Wouldn't put anything off—you know—like finishing school, or getting a job, or getting married and raising a family, or baby-sitting my grandkids, or ordering me a gravestone. Just stay cool. We'll get around to you."

He sketched a negligent salute, and the gravel rattled behind the wheels as he took off with Jud watching in a state of bemusement. Within seconds the gravel crunched and the car skidded to a halt, a tan-clad arm shot out and made circular waving motions. Puzzled but cooperative, Jud trotted forward and once more looked into the blue-gray eyes beneath the fiery hair.

"Had a thought. Could be you've got the makings of a good cop. It's not a bad life. Pay's lousy, but you get to tote a gun, ride around in cars a lot. Everybody loves you —even when you're gunning 'em down." He jerked a thumb toward the Burger Bin. "And you get to eat in all the best restaurants. Keep it in mind!" A wave, another rattle of gravel, and he was gone.

Jud stared after him, feeling somewhat the way a person does when he steps off a roller coaster—a little unsteady, a little disoriented. But good. *Real* good.

It was on the twenty-second of July, just short of three weeks later, when the strange package arrived in the mail. Jud would never forget the date because it was the day Victoria Jean Linden was born in the hospital at Grant's Pass between five and six a.m.

Jud and Bo came home in the pickup at midmorning, leaving Dad to take the bus or phone for a ride. Arriving, he didn't stop at the mailbox at the foot of the front sidewalk because he seldom thought about it, not being on anyone's mailing list except Snory's. But while he was having a snack he remembered Dad was expecting a good-size check.

Bo volunteered as usual to help out and they walked down to the box. It contained the usual mixture of things to keep and things to throw away. And it contained the package, which certainly didn't look like something anybody would want. More or less in the shape of a box, it was wrapped in brown paper that had once been a Safeway bag.

He put it on the kitchen table along with the rest of the

things for Dad to sort through, and was about to go outside again, when something about the address caught his eye. It was printed with a soft pencil in large capital letters and it didn't say Victor Linden, or V. C. Linden, it said J. LINDEN. There was no return address. He picked it up again, hefted it, shook it. It didn't rattle, nor did it weigh much.

It had to be for him. No other J. LINDEN around. It looked like somebody's idea of a joke. Well okay, he'd go along. He tore off the paper which was secured only by bits of tape here and there and a string he broke easily with his hands. The flimsy box inside nearly fell apart with no help from him. It was a minor miracle the post office had even accepted it.

He stared, totally blank one moment and totally comprehending the next. Inside was a beat-up, dented, aluminum saucepan with a handle, and there wasn't a doubt in the world who had sent it. Taped to the inside bottom of the pan was a folded sheet of paper and in a moment he was reading the message:

THOT HE WOOD MISS THIS I MISS HIM BUT HES BETR OFF YRS TRULY YVONNE PS I TURNT HIM LOSE BULL HE WAS MAD AS FAR WHICH I DONT BLAME HIM I GUESS I WILL REMEMBER BO AND YOU

His thoughts far away in time and dimension, Jud smoothed the paper and folded it methodically, like an automaton, and put it on a stairstep to take up to his room later, then he picked up the pan and wandered vaguely out into the back yard, glad that he didn't have to talk to anybody right then. Just as vaguely he sat in the old tire swing that still hung from a limb of the huge cherry tree that must have been there about a hundred years. Putting the pan down, he sat there making the tire sway a little from side to side while he tried not to imagine what Bull must have done to her when he was "mad as far." He thought too of the lengths to which she must have gone to wrap the pan and smuggle it into town when she got the chance, and to mail it without Bull's finding out.

While he sat there Bo came ambling around from the front of the house, spotted him, and came up at a trot. He saw the pan at once and nosed it a little, wagging his tail. Then he looked up at Jud—gratefully, it seemed. "Don't look at me," Jud murmured. "I didn't give it to you. Present from an old friend. Your best friend ever, maybe."

A moment later he slid out of the tire and down to his knees where he grabbed a handful of the rufflike folds of loose hide on either side of Bo's neck and roughly shook the big head from side to side. "You big moose," he said, "you think you're worth all the headaches you've been to your friends?"

Bo sat down, hitched himself about six inches closer, tail sweeping the grass behind him, and grinned a smug, wet grin, implying that he certainly did.